# FINAL DIAGNOSIS

# FINAL DIAGNOSIS

## Book 1 | No Second Chances

## J. T. Madicus

## Illustrated by Gabriel Rodak

# CONTENTS

CHAPTER I

# CHECK
# YOUR DIAGNOSIS

ALL GOOD THRILLERS START WITH a bang. A gunshot. An explosion. A beautiful woman. But on the day this saga begins, I wake to the sound of a knock on the front door. Three loud thumps that rip me from an uneasy sleep. I have no friends ... as far as I remember. People dislike me, but few hate me enough to come knocking in person at such an ungodly hour of noon. A shot of whiskey sits on my nightstand. Life is short, so why not start the day with a proper breakfast? I down the whiskey in one swig. There can only be one person knocking at this hour.

I hear the front door unlock and I smell coffee. Instinctively, my mouth waters. Breakfast is here. Well, lunch. Lunch with a side of guilt. Phil is his name. Phil the pill man. Or did I just make that up? Whatever his name, he complains about being forced to make deliveries to me—especially deliveries of a certain controlled substance. A simple pharmacist, but, unfortunately for him, a foolish man. At least I didn't cheat on my wife with a prostitute. Not that I have a wife. What I do have is a never-ending supply of orange bottles containing small, white pills. They look like over-the-counter painkillers. But you can't get these over the counter.

Friends come and go, and we all know where we fit in; I am no one's friend, but everyone has their value and I always get what I want. Usually, it is the satisfaction of being right. This time, it's small rounds of beautifully crafted, pharmaceutical-grade opium. Bon appetit.

Tiffany disapproves. She's ... well, she's the employee, with an ample supply of skills. I pay her to keep me alive—better yet, to make me feel alive, at which she succeeds—and to keep me sane, at which she fails. She is the whisperer of sweet nothings in my ears, the provider of tender touch that melts away all the pain. She provides a good service—the girlfriend experience with the voice in my head that most people are born with. The one that tells you to brush your teeth before bed. To call your mother on her birthday. To pay your bills before the IRS knocks on your door. To take your medicine before bed. Apparently, most people think of these things by themselves. I don't. Hence Tiffany. But she doesn't seem to be here today.

No sooner has Phil scuttled away when my door once again clicks open. Another person strolls in off the street like he's family. He brandishes a soggy sandwich and healthy stack of mail. Oh, will someone just punch away that look on his face! Pity ... some contempt? No. Fear. Fear and sadness. Ughh! Disgusting combination. The hour goes by with Jeff. Fortunately he only visits once a month. Since there's no TV to stare at or WiFi to dive into, we are forced to interact. It's brief and awkward. He sorts through the mail and tosses the New England Journal of Medicine at me. I'm sitting up in bed, surrounded by stacks of JAMA (Journal of the American Medical Association), BMJ (British Medical Journal) and of course my favorite, the NEJM. I take the proffered sandwich and eat in silence, contemplating suicide. Oh don't be so dramatic! You would be suicidal too if you ended up in Mississippi, one of the cheapest states to live in. The South with its "Southern charm." Jeff seems to have left. Now I'm alone. Just one of these pills to help me deal with Jeff, another to take the edge off the day and another … well, why not? It's so hard to count when you're sober, isn't it? Good night, dear reader. Tomorrow will probably be the same. I wonder what Phil will bring for lunch.

The room is cold. The air tastes strange. Something has changed. My head throbs, but not in the usual way. Something is different. My eyes still shut, I notice that I'm sitting up. The chair is soft, and moves gently below me as I shift in the seat. Did I fall asleep at my desk? No, it's a hospital wheelchair. If you'd lived the kind of life I have, you'd recognize it too.

I feel a sharp, metallic coldness on each of my wrists. Handcuffs. Kinky, in other circumstances, but right now downright inconvenient. I open my eyes. The room is dark. I squint. Lifting my cuffed hands to my face like a goddamned rabbit, I rub my eyes. Images swim before me.

A light clinks on, for a moment blinding me, before revealing a cold room. No natural light. A single bulb hanging down from the ceiling. The light is not bright, but my eyes still sting from the change. Before me is a metal desk. On it sit four iPads, a glass pitcher of water, and four empty glasses.

The pills I took the night before—or whenever that was—are beginning to wear off. I find myself sober, hand-cuffed, sitting in a wheelchair in a dimly lit room. The walls are concrete, the humidity is high, the temperature is cold. I am underground. Things could be better. Maybe I am dead and this is hell. Well, at least it's quiet. At least I'm alone. Four iPads though ... that is not a good sign.

"Diagnose the patient, Doctor Tseng, and earn your freedom." The voice echoes in the small room. Distorted, artificial. And bloody annoying. I should be scared, but when you are this hungover, it doesn't matter. Behind me a door opens. A guard—hulking, pale, expression-less—walks in, wheeling before him a slumped figure in a wheelchair. The unfortunate prisoner is parked beside me, facing the table. I say "facing," but it's hard to tell when somebody has a sack over their head.

The guard leaves, and another follows, pushing an-other captive, head covered like the last one. This guard exits, and yet another walks in! Is it my birthday? No. The liquid in the pitcher is most certainly not vodka. This isn't a party.

The final guard removes the sacks from each prisoner in turn. A blonde woman. Quite fetching. Cuffed like me, squinting into the light. A bulky, square-jawed man, who glares at the guard. And finally, a dark-skinned man with a gentle face who looks around curiously, taking in the whole scene. Both men have bruises and cuts on their faces, as though they have been roughed up a bit. The blonde is the first to speak:

"What time is it? Where are we?" Of course the woman speaks first.

"Interesting that you want to know the time of day before finding out where you are," I say, but I do add helpfully, "In either case, I don't know."

The distorted voice speaks again. Can I hear evidence of a slight smile, buried below the layers of electronic distortion?

"Welcome, doctors. I'd like you to meet Doctor Tseng. This will be his home for a while. It doesn't have to be yours. I hear he's not a good roommate. Before you is a conundrum. Solve it for me, and you will earn your freedom."

The iPads light up. I look around. The blonde has somehow removed a hairpin, and is fidgeting with her handcuffs, trying to pick the lock. Her hair is falling across her face.

"Are you going to keep staring at me, or are you going to help us get out of here?" As the woman speaks again, I try to place the accent. American, with a rough, aggressive tone. Possibly New England. Most likely New York.

Her cuffs click open. They fall off and dangle on the arm of her wheelchair. She passes her hairpin to the bulky man sitting next to her. Surely these guys can't be much use here! What about the third bloke. Dark, thin, looks a bit ill. Bet he's quick with the hairpin though. Hmmm, maybe that's why I don't have any friends? People often say I'm offensive. I wonder why … Anyway, my head is starting to throb more. Focus, I tell myself. Let's get out of here. The less time with this circus, the better.

My hands are bound tight together, but I can still reach forward. Assuming my amnesia is due to a heavier-than-usual dose of drugs, I reach forward and clumsily grasp at the water on the table. Better start flushing the system.

The muscular man picks up an iPad and begins to read. "Patient is a 35-year-old male with undulant fever, fatigue, and an enlarged spleen. Current diagnosis is chronic fatigue syndrome." Time to take control. I never was a patient man.

"What do you think, Muscles?" I ask the man holding the iPad. "Well, yeah. Undulant fever. Fatigue. Enlarged spleen. It fits." Apparently he is an idiot. Maybe the blonde has brains? "Blondie?" I say. She sits up and takes charge.

"The patient is male. Most chronic fatigue syndrome patients are women. Why are we playing this sick game anyway?"

She has some knowledge, but ultimately fails to deliver. "Nice pun," I say.

It's always a painful thing, to watch a beautiful woman roll her eyes. Anyway, speaking of pain, I am always in pain. I am always tired. I want out and to be home in my flat. And of course, I want my pills. I reach into my pocket, praying the pills are there. I'm even starting to miss Jeff. Let's get this riddle solved. Lucky for the patient, one pill is there. I take it out and pop it into my mouth. Time to shine my light on this mystery.

"Syndromes are used by incompetent doctors who are unable to find a real diagnosis," I say. "Let's actually think here. What causes chronic fatigue syndrome?"

"Lyme disease," says the thin man. His voice is soft, almost feminine.

"No maculopapular rash," I say, trying to keep the disappointment out of my voice, but not trying too hard. "Look at his history. He'd been on a ton of antibiotics recently, yet he's still ill." The woman leans forward. "What about brucellosis? The patient has an undulant fever, the infection affects both men and women, and could also lead to enlargement of the spleen."

Now it is my turn to roll my eyes at her, which annoys her. The muscular man interjects, reading from the iPad.

"The patient has lactose intolerance, so exposure to milk or dairy products containing Brucella is pretty unlikely."

"What if he was exposed to them unwittingly?" she says. I pick up an iPad, and read through the text.

"You missed something," I say, looking first at the muscular man to my left, between me and the woman, and next at the thin, dark-skinned man to my right. "The patient was admitted to a hospital two weeks ago. If it were a simple brucellosis infection, it would have resolved by now, and we wouldn't have the pleasure of this meeting."

"What about the enlarged spleen? Only a handful of diseases cause this," says the blonde woman, tapping her iPad with a carefully trimmed nail.

"Only a handful? How medically precise. You sure you're a doctor?"

"Top of my class at Harvard," she retorts, scrolling through the text on the iPad. "The patient lived in Prague for three years. He has slightly elevated cholesterol levels, slightly elevated alanine transaminase and aspartate transaminase levels. Oh … naughty boy. He contracted chlamydia three years ago and was treated with azithromycin."

"He's clearly an alcoholic and a slut—brilliant diagnosis," I snap. That was harsh; I must be hungry.

"It could be Lyme disease," the woman says as she looks at the man across from her, trying to figure out who this skinny black man is. She is probably desperately reaching for any diagnosis that will get her out of this situation. I can see the frustration on her face.

"What about lupus?" the muscular man pipes in.

"It's NEVER lupus!" the dark-skinned man exclaims. "I think it is thalassemia."

Finally! He has something correct to say, and says it with power and passion. Maybe he is not as useless as I thought.

9

"A little too focused on the spleen, aren't we?" I say, glancing at Mr. Muscles. "What did I tell you about syndromes? Lupus is a diagnosis of exclusion. All that muscle and no brain!" That'll show 'em. Oops, Muscles isn't happy. In fact, he is red with anger. I probably shouldn't be pissing off a guy who outweighs me and has biceps bigger than my thigh!

"Look, Mr. Tseng. Or Dr. Tseng. Or whatever your name is," snaps the blonde. "It's DEFINITELY Lyme disease. Okay. So we have our diagnosis. Can we go now, please?" She stares at the ceiling where the distorted voice was coming from.

Oh if only patience was a virtue—then again, I am not a virtuous man. I can be rude. I can stereotype. I can cause offense. But those who put up with this know that more often than not … well, let me show you. Hopefully, my new "friends" will learn too. "You have no life!" I shout. The blonde recoils in her chair, looking shocked. "It is not Lyme disease! You said it yourself: the patient lived in Prague. When have you seen wildlife in Prague?" I look around the room at the stunned faces and continue: "What happened when you all woke up here? None of you wept. None of you screamed. Not one of you begged for your freedom. You didn't even look surprised! What does this mean? It's clear that there's nothing waiting for any of you back at home."

Silence. Why does this always happen after I speak? Ah well, in for a penny, in for a pound …

"None of you have any life. Sure, you have some medical knowledge, but it's clear that none of you have practiced in the last five years. Let's see, what do we have here?

"Girl doctor with trimmed nails, straight permed hair. Five-inch stiletto heels. Looking good without makeup, even in captivity. Beautiful, confident, and aggressive. You are definitely from Harvard as you claim. You may have even been at the top of your class. But not in medicine. Computer science?"

A defiant stare. Not a trace of hurt. I know I'm right. Muscles should be an easier one to solve. I turn to him.

"Meathead. Well groomed but still stuck in the golden years of your lost prime. The suit is from the 90s and your hair, well … Sure, you were a jock and the ladies couldn't resist your biceps and your charm. You did study medicine. Maybe you even practiced, for a time. But that's not who you are now. No doctor would wear that suit. Your whole look is designed not only to impress, but also to ingratiate. You need people to like you, but not for long. You're a salesman. Used cars? After this we should talk. You can prescribe me a new ride."

"How about I just punch you in the face?" Muscles says. "I worked the streets of Chicago. I've watched men die many times. Who do you think you are to dictate the value of a life?"

"Now now, Muscles. We're all in this together. Speaking of … YOU!"

I turn to the final person in the room. The slim man looks at me calmly, without fear. The muscular man fumes silently to my left but still listens, curious to learn about his fellow prisoner. I knew that would be easy. But what are we in for now?

"You. Slim ... very slim. Even sickly. Quiet, reserved, only giving input when needed, not concerned about being the loudest voice in the room. You're an introvert, and you're clever. Your appearance is polished with everything in its proper place. Not a single strand of hair is out of place, despite the rough treatment you had getting here. Your suit is perfect. Your boots polished. But there's a speck of dirt on your left heel. You know this. You've been glancing at it constantly, desperate to take it off and give it a polish. You have OCD. You have no job and are currently living in the basement of your mother's home ..."

The thin man flashes me a look. Some small detail out of place? He would hate that. But my diagnosis is accurate.

"Okay, until recently you were living in the basement of your mother's home. Things changed for you recently. Your mother loved you. But your father walked out when you came of age. Since then, you've been trying to make everything perfect. You blame yourself for his leaving. You know rationally that it's not your fault. But you feel guilt. Guilt about something. You think some aspect of yourself caused your father to walk out ... your sexuality. Oh, you poor thing! And now you have committed yourself to doing good. Good grief."

That's the three of them. Solved. Humans are like illnesses. Everyone has cause for how they are now. The difference is there's usually no cure.

"Well done, well done," says the blonde woman drolly. "You've figured out all of us. But have you figured out this patient? Regardless of what you say, I do want to go. I do have places to be. If you're so brilliant, solve this problem and let's go."

The other two doctors nod in agreement. Sycophants. There's a moment of silence, and then the familiar, distorted voice blares down from the ceiling.

"Oh, they were right about you, Dr. Tseng! I am definitely keeping you. As for the rest of you ... no. No, I'm afraid you're staying here too. You see, our Tseng needs an audience. He needs people to impress. And you, unfortunately, are the audience he needs."

"We need to eat!" snaps the blonde. "And I need to make a phone call. I don't know who you are. I don't know where we are. I don't know who HE is"—she points at me—"but we have rights. You can't just keep us here."

"Very well. I have no use for dead doctors. The water on the table is pure. And you shall have what you asked for. And when you have your final diagnosis, you will go free. You have my word." The blonde snorts and runs her fingers through her hair. The muscular man stands and kicks the wall. He sits down with a sigh, burying his face in his hands. The thin doctor just sits there silently, staring into space. I read through the iPad, searching for clues.

With a creak, the heavy door slides open, and a guard appears. He passes around four pizza boxes, still hot, and hands a mobile phone to the blonde who snatches it out of his hand. He turns to leave but pauses, and pats his inside pocket. He takes out a small, orange pill bottle, and hands it to me, his face expressionless. "She says you might need these."

She?

Glancing sadly at the soggy pizza, I hear a dial tone and the beep of numbers being entered into a phone. There's no ring. An automated voice comes out of the phone, audible to all of us. It's in an unfamiliar language. Not German. Not Russian, but Slavic. It could be Polish, or Slovak. I glance at the pizza box. On top in big orange letters is written "PizzaPraha."

"So," I say, unscrewing the lid on the pill bottle. "I guess we're in the Czech Republic! Vítejte."

A few pills, a few slices of pizza, and some water. It's not a party. But it could be worse. This wheelchair ain't so bad, once you get used to it. The room is getting dark again.

# CHAPTER II

# FROM PRAGUE WITH LOVE

THE OLD TOWN OF PRAGUE. Nighttime. Those winding streets, the dominating castle, streetlamps illuminating the footsteps of revellers: old-time locals staggering out of the pivovarnia (beer halls), their faces coated in sweat, insides bloated and greasy. Backpackers, tourists and foreign students mingling with the young locals in the bars and clubs. Faint tang of weed smoke in the air, and the moon hangs low above Karlův Most, otherwise known as the Charles Bridge. The buskers have gone home, and Joe is walking purposefully toward the town center, clutching his cell phone, guided by his Tinder account across the medieval city. Irina looks even more stunning in person. That red dress, necklace that draws the eye, just teasing the line of her bust. Blonde hair, blue eyes, and a smile that is simultaneously an invitation and a challenge. Joe cannot believe his luck. She likes his confidence, that American charm. Economics student, too. Though isn't he a bit old to be studying? Still, he has moves. Drinks. Shots. Maybe some pills? Nothing they haven't done before. A kiss in the bar. Your place or mine? Counting down the minutes until the Uber arrives. Dawn illuminates the ancient city. Tomorrow. A kiss goodbye. Another date. A couple of selfies. Chemistry fades. They both move on.

The light flicks on. The floor is hard beneath me. I find myself in a bright cafe and not a dark basement. I remember the basement, but whatever pills they gave me, they are good. So where was I? Ah yes, the Czech Republic. Lunatic disembodied voice and circus party of non-doctor doctors diagnosing a mystery man on an iPad. How long have I been asleep for? Again, must have been those pills. Pretty good hospitality, considering. Anyway, where is my coffee?

"Good morning, Tseng!" The blonde. A bit smiley, a bit too cheerful—but I am not complaining. Sitting with the others, businesslike around a table in a cafe, each holding an iPad, scrolling through details on our dear patient sipping on their morning joe. Is that a croissant? Okay, enough, don't overplay the delusions. And who says "good morning" these days, anyway?

"Any new ideas?" I say, asserting control.

"It could be thalassemia," repeats the thin man with conviction. "Patient has an enlarged spleen, so it's possibly a genetic disorder that's causing his chronic fatigue." I like him; he might just be my star pupil, and he is so convincing in his conviction, but he missed something and I unfortunately will have to ruin his dream. Apparently, they didn't get any smarter during my nap, I see, but they are coming up with better suggestions. Still, the thin man doesn't waste his words.

I politely reply. I am never polite—but this is my hallucination, not theirs. "It's not thalassemia," I say, "but not a bad diagnosis. Look at his blood work."

"Blood is normal with no elevated ferritin levels," Muscles replies, but this time without a smirk. Maybe I was wrong with my preconceptions about him.

"Is there a tox-screen on the patient?" I ask. I am thinking the drugs might have fried his system. Believe me, I know how that feels.

The muscular doctor answers … now in a British accent. Did he always talk like this?

"Yes—negative for any drugs. But the patient is a heavy drinker. Fatty liver. Liver disease would cause insomnia, leading to daytime somnolence. It must be fatty liver disease."

Ah … I like this cafe! Even my colleagues seem like tolerable, even pleasant, company. But this place seems all too familiar. Have I been here before? Something is not right, but that doesn't matter right now. Push it away, Tseng. There'll be a reckoning later, no doubt.

"Sorry, too much time in the gym, and not enough in the library, Handsome." Wait—did I just call him handsome?

"Blondie, tell him he's an idiot, and give us the benefit of your opinion," I say, reverting to form.

"He's right," she says. "You're an idiot."

Was that a slight wink in my direction? Focus, Tseng. "Patient has slightly elevated ALT/AST levels and the CT scan only shows mildly fatty liver, most likely due to heavy drinking," she says. "You're right, Tseng. It's not the liver."

"Say that again, but slower." "It's not the liver?"

Shit, I overplayed my hallucination; I am back in the basement, but the cafe mirage was a nice mental break from reality. Huh, my handcuffs are off. My new friends' wrists are uncuffed, too. That makes life more comfortable. The blonde is quite fetching, so maybe I should make the best of this situation. Time to be "nice."

"No," I say. "Never mind. Look. You may actually be alright. Maybe it's a good thing"—I turn to Blondie—"that your get-out-of-jail phone call failed. What happened when you tried to use that cell phone?"

"A voice in Czech, I think. I'm not good at languages, but I guess it was saying no international calls allowed."

"Convenient. No local friends?" "Afraid not."

"Come on, Tseng. You're supposedly the genius here. Why don't you solve it?" says the muscular man. I knew the time would come when he would challenge me. His mistake.

"Okay, Muscles, keep your biceps on. We don't know enough." Muscles, sensing weakness, exclaims, "But everything is here!" "No. Not about the patient. About the person. We need to know what he was doing before he got sick. We need to get to know the man behind the mystery."

Let's see what I can do with this iPad. I read.

Patient is in his mid 30s. Male, dark hair, green eyes, tall. Heavy drinker who is sexually active. He has lived in many countries with his most recent location being

Prague, Czech Republic. Patient is an international student from Texas studying economics. No major illness or surgeries. Chief complaint is severe fatigue to the point he is unable to get out of bed, except to use the bathroom and eat.

Something oddly familiar is stirred within me as I read the history. But why? Do I relate to this patient, or do I envy him and wish I were him? Well, why else would you get up except to use the bathroom and eat anyway? I fiddle with the device, but it's locked. No browser. No social media. No email. It's time to talk to the gods.

"Hey you—Voice in the Sky," I say. "We need to know more about this guy we're meant to be curing. We don't even know his name. Something happened in Prague that caused his illness. We need social media STAT. We need a better history on this guy. Let's see what's going on."

Silence. God's away on business? But no. The heavens are merciful, after all. My iPad goes blank, and starts to reset. It opens, logged into a Facebook account of a Nathan Whipton. Oh, well played, disembodied voice man!

"Hey, one of you kids come use this and find out about this mysterious Texas Ranger looking fellow," I say. "Search his friends. Look at his pictures. Read his past messages. Basically, do the spy stuff that you see on TV."

"You've got Facebook," says the blonde, snatching the iPad. "Give that here. I'm going to get us out of here!"

Just then, the light in the room flicks off. The distorted voice echoes down: "Not so fast, sweetie. We know you are a very good hacker and we've made sure we disabled geolocation, so give up your foolish efforts at escape. I thought there might be a need to talk to some people out of the room in order to get your diagnosis, so I've taken the liberty of making Nathan's account available for you. He is a friend of the patient. I also have a whole team monitoring your every keystroke. One false move and the connection will be cut, and I will have you handcuffed again. Yes, I know you picked your handcuffs. Better yet, a straightjacket may make all of you more compliant."

The light returns. The blonde looks angry, but determined. She hands the iPad to Muscles. "Go for it, pretty boy."

I sit in my wheelchair and watch him from across the table as he searches. "You're not here to check out the girls," says the thin man, but without a trace of anger in his voice. "Focus."

Muscles flashes a guilty smile and swipes at the iPad.

"Ah, here we go," he says. "Ladies and gentlemen, we have our man! Patient is Joe Travis from Austin, Texas. Let's have a look at his wall. Nothing for the last three months, but before then he posted quite frequently—selfies from Prague, beers with mates. Just before things went quiet, he posted a few photos with a girl. Wow!" Joe, dark, tall, handsome in a conventional way, is sitting at a classic Czech bar, pilsner in one hand and a cigarette in the other, staring with casual confidence at the lens. Next to him sits ... well, I told you I liked blondes, and this one is exceptional. Sorry, Doctor Blonde, you're hot, sure, but

23

this chick. Wow. Piercing blue eyes. Luscious hair. And further down … well, I think my diagnosis is obvious. Why am I envious of this patient? Tseng, snap out of it! What else can you observe? Joe is smoking Lucky Strikes. Maybe we'll strike lucky? Move on.

"Yeah, yeah, she's hot; come on, boys, focus," the blonde snaps us to attention. I think Muscles may have drooled a little. The thin man seemed disinterested. He, I assume, is more interested in Joe or at least diagnosing him.

"Look!" he says. "He looks great in this photo with the girl. But then she disappears. Next photo is with a few classmates. It's only one week later, but he looks awful. Sunken eyes. Pale face. Noticeably thinner."

"Hyperthyroidism?" says the blonde.

I ignore her and say, "Go to the girl's page." I find her more interesting.

"Same photo with Joe. Nothing until about two weeks later. And then there she is. Her usual healthy self. So maybe she got ill and lay low for a bit, but then got better. Joe, on the other hand, stayed sick," says Muscles.

"So they both got ill, but how?" says the blonde. "One way to find out. Give it here, kids," I say.

Muscles reluctantly gives me the iPad, and I start typing a message to Irina, the blonde who was in the same picture as Joe. Hey, it's Nathan, I'm a friend of Joe's from America. He talked about you all the time! Are you his girlfriend? I'm flying to Prague tomorrow to visit him but he's not answering his phone and I can't get a hold of him. Do you have any idea where he is?

To my surprise, moments later, Irina starts typing. She does not sound happy. Girlfriend! Hah! We party together a few months ago. I think he was nice boy but he gives me the chlamydia. If you find him, tell him to never write to me again. Stupid slutty Americans.

"Must say, they're rather direct, these Czechs," says the blonde. "What chicks?" Muscles asks, a stupid look on his face. "Czechs!" the blonde says. I wouldn't tell a stranger I've never met that I got an STD off their friend."

"A stranger you've never met? That's a tautology. Anyway, focus. Look at this photo," I say, taking charge again and pointing to a bland selfie of the man.

"Has he been tested for other STDs such as HIV?" the thin black man pipes in.

Muscles is quick to interject, "I don't think Joe is gay, black, or from Africa."

Wow, that was harsh, but Muscles doesn't see what I see. There is a reason why our dark-skinned doctor friend is thin and it's not because he is gay or works out. He does have HIV. But he is not my patient right now. I ignore the comments and focus on the photo. Let's see if they see what I see.

"Ok people, LOOK at this photo!" I zoom in on the iPad, and the others lean closer. Now the blonde gets excited. It looks like she really might have some medical knowledge in her. "Look at his neck. He's thin, but there's a definite thickness here. His glands are swollen."

"It could be hypothyroidism," says Muscles.

"Again with the thyroids," I say. "It's definitely an infection and not hypothyroidism. Look, let's resolve this." I look at the ceiling.

"Hey, God! Run standard tests on thyroid function. Once they come back normal, do me a favor—send in your goons and handcuff her again for thinking hypothyroidism. I like my women to be bound and silent. Oh, and slap Muscles too for agreeing with her, would you?"

The blonde gets up and moves over to me. I am not intimidated. I've felt pain worse than what she can dish at me.

"If you are going to slap me, hurry up," I say, keeping my cool. I hope. "I am trying to diagnose this patient and I don't have time for childish tantrums."

Her face is inches away from mine, eyes piercing me with her stare. Am I confused, or am I in denial? Most women don't fancy me and I've had my share of slaps. She moves to straddle me as I sit in my wheelchair. Oh, this can't end well, but who cares? I return her stare, unflinching. Her face blocks my view of the other two, but I can only imagine their eyes watching what is about to happen. The blonde is clever. She whispers into my ear, "Why are you nervous? Just admit it, you like me." She sticks her tongue into my mouth. I am not saying I didn't enjoy it; she has a way with her tongue, and I return in kind as we play tonsil tennis. TONSILS—that's it! I try to push her off.

"Hey, Voice in the Sky, do a biopsy of his tonsils and, since we're in Prague, inject them with vodka, which will reduce the swelling and make them easier to remove."

"Very well. But you better be right, Doctor Tseng. I like you, but maybe they are wrong about you, and I am running out of patience," the voice booms.

I look at the blonde, who is still straddling me, and I wink. "Bet you've never met a doctor who can order up biopsies from the heavens before," I say. Wait, that sounded flirty and not arrogant. Ugh, Tseng, sometimes I don't even know who you are anymore.

She bends over and I can still smell the lingering trace of an expensive perfume. She kisses me deeply, again, right on the mouth. I feel my face flush. She stands, and returns to her seat knowing she has won in seducing me.

"No, Tseng," she says, "I don't think I've ever met a doctor like you before."

Composure. Composure. Come on, pull yourself together. It's just a kiss. You're not twelve. Come on. Down, boy. Focus. Ignoring the blonde as best I can, I look around the room at the other two doctors, who are staring at me with unabashed astonishment. "Come on, kids, we have work to do," I say. "Now, most of you Yanks don't know that there are two major strains of the Epstein-Barr virus that cause mononucleosis. The less virulent American strain and the more virulent European strain. Most people have their tonsils removed and are unaffected by either strain, but Joe kept his and his tonsils became the perfect home for it to survive and wreak havoc. Apparently, he gave her chlamydia, but she gave him the infectious mononucleosis which, as you should all know, is a form of herpes. So, lesson of the day: Be careful who you kiss."

"Now I'm regretting giving you that kiss!" the woman says. Very funny, blondie. I ignore her.

"You mark my words. Any moment that mystery voice is going to come back to say that."

My words are greeted by blank stares of … not agreement, not contradiction … but of something else.

"Alright, let's make a wager to make things interesting," I continue. "$50 says the tests will come back positive for Epstein-Barr. They'll remove the tonsils, and Joe will be right as rain."

Silence. Awkward silence. The thin doctor shuffles a bit, and glances at a speck on his shoe. The blonde hasn't looked at me in at least five minutes. Not that I've noticed. Muscles stares at me, considering calling me on the wager. He is a foolish man trying to be the leader, hoping by some miracle that I am wrong. But there is one problem: he doesn't have a diagnosis of his own, so to call me out would be too risky. Time to hurry this show up.

"Hey, I know you're up there. Got my test results? You know I'm right, and I know who you are. So come on. Let my people go!" I am not stupid, but I know there is a reason to everything. I call out, "Jeff, come out and reveal yourself! I know you are behind this."

Silence. And then that same voice.

"Very well, Doctor Tseng. You were right, of course, the pathologist has seen his infected cells through the microscope. Joe has received his injection of vodka to his tonsils and is on the road to recovery. And you are all free to explore the city. May I suggest a visit to the old town?

Just beware of the local girls … They bite. Tseng, I am also sending Jeff to you. I am sure you two have a lot to talk about."

The door clicks open. I pop a pill, but for a moment, no one stands up to leave.

# CHAPTER III

# DOCTOR DANGER

THERE, THAT WASN'T TOO HARD, was it? Chronic fatigue syndrome, I mean, really! Bright, this lot, but they lack imagination. They lack vision. Things look pretty good now. But they're going to get worse soon. How do I know this? I just do. I know things. That's the curse of being me. I am good at what I do. I figure people out; I have to. The person you meet can be the death of you or can be your savior.

Make the wrong friends and you end up in a grave. Make the right friends and you dodge a bullet. While I am right about 99% of the time, that other 1% happens because I miss the finer details of someone's life. I'm not talking about the mess. It's easy to tell when a person is damaged, and why. It is harder to know the gentler, more intimate details. What gets them up in the morning? Why do they bother? So here is what we know about my new "friends/colleagues."

Back in America, A Few Days Ago ...

The puddles in the street outside the diner glow red beneath a lone traffic light. The light flashes green, and most traffic hurtles forward. A black sedan is the one exception. It's past midnight, but the dark car glides forward with its lights off and parks on the curb beside the diner.

Inside the restaurant, a blonde woman sits by the window. She sips idly on a coffee and reads a book. A half-eaten plate of food sits in front of her. She ignores the ogling stares of the half-drunk male clientele. She appears to also ignore the black sedan pulling up right next to her window. But if you were watching closely, you'd notice her grip on her coffee mug tighten, her knuckles turn white. It's hard to tell if it's fear that you're observing, or anger, or both.

A tall, muscular man exits the car and strides into the diner. He looks around, surveying the room. He approaches the solitary woman. Without speaking, he takes a small, black phone out of his pocket and hands it to her. She stares him down for a moment, before putting down her coffee and calmly taking the phone. Others would be afraid in this situation. But the woman acts as if this kind of thing happens to her every day. Her eyes betray annoyance rather than fear. Her hands are quite steady. Silently, she puts it to her ear.

"I could have you killed. Right here, right now. But I'd rather make your life miserable." The voice of a mobster—to the point and with power.

"My life's already miserable," she replies.

"It could always be worse." His tone is sadistic.

The woman sighs and rolls her eyes at the mountainous man who handed her the phone and is listening intently to the audible half of the conversation.

"We've been through this," she says into the phone. "You can't touch me. I've hacked all your communications. You have the proof; I sent you the sample this morning. Now you know every morning I have to enter the code into my computer. If I don't, incriminating evidence gets sent to the State Police, plus a few friends at the FBI. And you know what I have. So what are you calling for?"

"Because I think you're bluffing."

"Fine. Kill me. I have nothing to lose, but you on the other hand ... if I die, you go down. Your organization will collapse. The supply of cheap fentanyl in New York, Los Angeles, Chicago and Baltimore will dry up. For a time, fewer kids will OD. Fewer families will be ruined."

The male voice on the other side replies after a moment's pause, his voice softer, almost charming, "What kind of arrangement can we agree on?"

"If I turned you in now, some other scumbag would take your place within a few months. You're more useful to me in the open. People who want to do drugs will always find a way. Criminals like you will keep coming until America's drug problem is killed at the source."

"Come now, little girl. I am not a Harvard grad like you, and I don't like lectures. You have us bent over a barrel. Or so you think. So I ask you for the final time ... what do you want?"

"The same thing as everyone else. Money. Fifty thousand U.S. dollars donated to Drug Free America every month in my name. Think of it as a tax-deductible donation."

"Very well. But we're not done with you, little lady. Your luck will run out eventually."

The line goes dead. Still calm, the woman tosses the phone back to the hulking man. He takes it and turns away without a word. The black sedan appears to glide off into the night. The woman sighs again and glances wearily at her coffee, which has gone cold. Slinging her bag over her shoulder, she drops a $20 bill on the counter and walks out the door.

It's started raining again, she thinks—a light drizzle, which distracts her for a moment. That is all it took. A strong arm grabs her around the neck. As she struggles to escape, another man rushes at her. She jerks her head back, smashing the nose of the first assailant. The second swings at her with a fist, but she kicks him in the groin and he goes down. The first man lunges at her again, his face covered in blood. She attacks him with an elbow, and stands over him as he falls.

The second assailant is still groaning in agony on the ground. The first is down, but appears composed. Bending over him, the woman recognizes him as the well-built thug who handed her the phone. An employee of the drug kingpin. Suddenly, rage swells up inside her. She extracts something small and metallic looking from her bag, and bends over the man on the ground. "Now," she says in a measured tone, "This won't hurt a bit."

She palpates his right clavicle, and makes a small incision with her scalpel. She then jams a small pick inside, slicing the nerves of the arm and ripping out red strips of sinew. The man howls in agony.

"Shut up now. You see, this is what happens when you underestimate a woman who has more balls and skills than most men. You will live. But you'll need a good microsurgeon if you ever want to use that arm again."

As the woman stands to leave, a black van screeches to a halt along the pavement. Three large men jump out, grab the woman, and pull her roughly into the back of the vehicle. The doors slam shut, and it roars away out of sight.

An interrogation room. Unlike the basement cell, this room is brightly lit, a government facility. There's an air of officialdom about the place. But sitting on the cold, metal chair, the woman from the diner still does not feel afraid. If anything, she feels bored.

"Can I at least get a coffee?" she says to the room at large. "Black, two sugars?" Silence.

The drill is as old as time. They may be cocky at first. But you make the subject wait. Their nerves get frayed. And then you walk in and offer relief. Respite from the bright lights. The uncertainty, that mix of pain and boredom, like a migraine that just won't cease. There's no clock in the room. Her phone is gone. She could have been there for minutes, hours or even days. Even highly trained minds get hysterical after a while.

After an immeasurable span of time, another woman walks in. She is tall and thin, with dark hair and of indeterminate age. She has the calm, authoritative demeanor of judge or a surgeon. "You have many aliases," she says.

The blonde woman looks up. "So would you if you were given a shit name and forced out of the house by your family when you were sixteen."

"Really!" says the dark-haired woman. "Wow, that almost made me cry. Save your sob stories, though. We know who you are, Margaret Jones. Or do you prefer Maggie?"

Sarcasm envelops sarcasm as the blonde replies, "I've always liked the name Elizabeth Brown. But you won't find it on your list. It looks like we're going to be getting to know each other pretty well in this lovely room, so how about you call me Liz."

"Liz then. Well, Liz, I am agent Thompson, but call me Tiffany. Would you like some water? A cigarette, perhaps? I believe you smoke Marlboro Red."

Liz takes the cigarette and lighter and lights it.

"You're not under arrest. You're not a bad person. You've broken some laws. But you did it for the right reasons." Tiffany glances down at a file, and continues, "Harvard-trained hacker. Taekwondo black belt since you were 17. Studied medicine but dropped out of your surgical fellowship. You're not easily intimidated. You've made some powerful enemies. And yet you've kept out of trouble, for the most part. Just two questions: Why did you drop out of your surgical fellowship and, more importantly, why do you hate drugs so much?"

"You cannot hold me against my will. I know my rights and I demand a phone call."

"You have conned powerful people. You've stolen millions." "I have conned criminals. I have stolen from thieves. I've given the money away."

"Yes, I know. A female Robin Hood. That's why you're here, and not in a real jail cell."

"I have brought down people who the police couldn't touch. You should be thanking me. Not making veiled threats."

"I don't make threats. You are not in America anymore. You are in the Czech Republic. Here, you have no rights. So please listen, and we can all get along. You didn't answer my question. Why do you hate drugs so much?"

Liz is getting angry now. Crossly, she replies, "Why are you asking me this?"

A look of amusement appears on Tiffany's face. "Our Doctor Tseng seems to love his drugs, and he washes down his pills with whiskey. Does that bother you?"

"I am not a foolish girl. I don't punish the victims; I punish the dealers. I just feel sorry for your Doctor Tseng."

A man walks into the room. One of his arms is in a sling. He is tall. It takes the dazed Liz a moment to recognize him as the same thug who assaulted her outside the diner.

"You've got some skills," he said. "The microsurgeon told me you made a perfect cut, not a vein or artery scratched. Still needs some more time to heal properly, but I will make a full recovery."

"Ah … thanks, I guess?"

Liz looked quizzically at the brown-haired woman.

"Meet Jim, he's one of ours. One year embedded in their organization." She looks now toward the man. "Is it done?"

"Yes ma'am." He looks toward Liz. "Your body was just discovered in the Hudson. Congratulations. This is the first day of the rest of your life."

"Join us, Liz," continues Tiffany. "We've blown up your old life. Your enemies are no longer hunting you. It was hard to watch you and keep track of you. Your recklessness in conning dangerous people made us think you were suicidal. Now, you have a second chance. We can help you apply your talents with more precision. Through us, you can do more good. You can help more people."

"Do I have a choice?"

"You can refuse. But you won't. We're offering you a chance to do the thing you love most in the world."

"Blackmail?"

"Medicine."

# CHAPTER IV

# DOCTOR DAMAGE

T HE CROWD IS THIRSTY FOR blood. His blood, his opponent's—it doesn't matter to them. He hears the roar from the stand. Blinking sweat out of his eyes, he flexes those muscular arms, and lunges toward his foe. The other combatant is smaller, wiry. Pitch-black eyes, and the quick, jerky movements of someone accustomed to danger. This man fights dirty.

A hard swing from the muscular fighter, but the small man ducks and aims a swift kick at his opponent's groin. He deflects the blow just in time. That would have been nasty. Time to end this fast. The small man is quick, but the larger fighter doesn't just have strength. He has brains. Eight years of medical training doesn't only teach a man how to heal. It also teaches how to injure.

Both fighters huddle in close, each searching for an opening. The small man attacks with his elbows. The larger fighter seizes his chance. He throws the other fighter against the walls of the cage and lands three swift, perfectly aimed blows around the chest and neck. The small fighter blinks, looking stunned. He then collapses to the ground.

The crowd roars. Bloodthirsty screams. But the noise begins to fade. The excitement turns to an anxious hush. The small man is writhing on the ground. His lips are turning blue. He clutches desperately at his throat before passing out. His heaving chest ceases to move. The large fighter shoves away the panic-stricken referee and begins to administer CPR. But it's too late.

The crowd has realized what happened. There is an angry mob approaching the fighter. This can't end well for him. The fighter continues to administer CPR when suddenly three tall, menacing men in suits race toward the ring.

Strong hands grab the muscular fighter and rip him off the still body. One of the suited men flings the muscled fighter over his shoulders as if he were a pillow, hurls open the door of the cage and hurries out, waving a handgun to ward off the wrath of the crowd. The back door of the arena is flung open, and the muscular fighter is dumped unceremoniously onto the ground.

He staggers to his feet in a fury. A shirt is thrown to him. "What the fuck is going on?" he asks. "I won your goddamn fight. Now let me go home."

"You nearly caused a fucking riot. Word of this is going to get out. People will be out for revenge. The boss won't be happy."

The fighter spits into the face of his captor, who responds with a firm slap. "Watch it! We don't need you. You owe us."

"I killed that man. I'm done fighting for you. I'm going home." A steel blade flashes in the dark. Two of the suited

43

men grab the fighter by the arms, while the other holds the knife to his neck. "What do you think, boys? Looks like the boss wants to cut his losses with him. Besides, the doctor should get the justice he deserves. Doesn't the bible say, a life for a life?"

Foolish thugs, they underestimate the power of a man when adrenaline is coursing through his body.

Three punches fly out faster than a blink. The knife clatters to the ground. One by one, the suited men collapse. The fighter looks around in horror. A van roars up. No time to think; the fighter starts to run. A woman holding a pistol jumps down, but upon hearing sirens, jumps back into the van. The fighter continues to run, but he is soon surrounded by police.

Bound in handcuffs and hunched in the back of a police cruiser, the fighter resigns himself to his fate. But suddenly the van roars out of nowhere and punches into the police cruiser with relentless speed. The woman jumps down from the van and flings a sack over the fighter's head. She drags him out of the cruiser and hurls him inside the van with astonishing strength. The van speeds away into the darkness.

"Who the fuck …!" The man starts to struggle, but a quick blow to the head from the butt of the pistol shuts him up. "Shhhh now," the woman says, giving the man an injection in the shoulder. "We're your friends. But you don't know it yet. And your temper is legendary. You'll understand soon enough."

It's still dark when the fighter wakes up. The sack over his head is gone, but he can see nothing beside the road except tall grass and weeds. The van turns off the highway onto a dirt road, and heads toward what looks like an abandoned airfield. A paved runway stretches off toward the horizon. The woman speaks into her cellphone, and lights appear on either side of the asphalt. A lean, military-style jet starts rolling toward them.

Grabbing the dazed fighter by the shirtfront, the woman leans in close and says, "Now, are you gonna comply, or am I going to have to give you another jab?" Anger flares up in the fighter, but subsides. This time, for once, he knows when he's beaten.

The van parks beside the airplane, and two men frogmarch the fighter inside. Although austere from the outside, the jet is luxurious inside. Leather seats, even a mini bar. An attractive stewardess hands the weary fighter a drink, saying, "Johnnie Walker Black on the rocks, sir, just how you like it. Now pick a seat and put your belt on. We're about to take off."

The sun has yet to appear. The plane charges down the runway and takes off. In the pitch black, it's impossible for the fighter to know if they're heading east or west. His captors have all thrown on blankets and sleeping masks. It seems like they're settling in for a long journey.

"Some fighters go for the head," Tiffany says, standing over the fighter. "Others go for the gut."

He blinks rapidly in the harsh, bright lights. His hands lie limp on his lap. Before him is a white table, and the tall woman who'd kidnapped him from outside the cage. It is clear that she's the one in control.

"You zeroed in on the vagus nerve," she goes on. "Did you have any military training?"

"Hey beautiful, I'd rather talk about you than the fight," he says.

"Sure thing, handsome," she replies calmly. "I am Agent Thompson, but you can call me Tiffany. Now that introductions are out of the way, would you rather talk about the diagnosis?"

"I'd rather talk about why on earth I'm in Prague with a bunch of strange doctors and that pill-popping lunatic."

"Ah, of course. You want to know about Tseng."

"It must be a setup. No one can diagnose a patient that fast without even meeting him … not even God!"

"You haven't seen anything yet. We believe that you, too, have great potential. And Tseng needs you as much as we need him. Now, don't you want to know about the man you attacked back in Chicago?"

"Is he dead?"

"Your punches triggered a heart attack. You attempted

CPR, but it failed. He's dead. Murder in an illegal cage fighting ring. You have truly fallen far, doctor."

"I'm not a doctor."

"No. But you were. Or, you should have been. You were a talented physician until you decided to punch your superior in the face. Maybe he deserved it. He suffered a black eye and a broken cheekbone. You lost your career. Soon the debt from your student loan started piling up, and you took on a job as a medic driving an ambulance. But the streets of Chicago are deadly and you were always first to arrive to attend the gunshot wounds of the victims. One time, you saw something you shouldn't have. The mob took you in and kept you alive, safe from the gangs, and paid off your loans. A loan from the mob came with strings attached. They used you as their own private doctor. Because of your size, and for their own amusement, they set you up as a rooster in their underground cock-fighting ring. After today's performance, they'll be after you harder than ever. No doubt someone called the police. They'll be after you too. Trust me, here is the safest place you've been for a while."

"You seem to know an awful lot about me. FBI, CIA?"

"Let's just say we're your guardian angels. We can give you your life back. A chance to press the reset button. To be who you could have been."

"What do you want?"

"Five years. Five years during which you will do what you were born to do. After that, we wipe the slate clean. A new name. A new identity. A fresh start. We can even give you a medical license. You will be able to practice again. Your loans cleared. Your future intact."

"What about justice for the man that I killed?" The woman laughs, a dry, humorless chuckle.

"There is no justice in the world, doctor," she says. They look into each other's eyes, and her voice softens.

"There is no justice," she repeats. "But there is redemption. You are of no use to the world in a cell. But through us, you can do what you were born to do."

"You want me to hurt people," says the man, looking down at the desk before him.

"No, we want you to heal. Heal others, and through this work, you will heal yourself."

The woman slides a contract and pen across the table. The man picks up the pen, and then hesitates.

"I don't work well with others and I definitely will not work for—or under—Tseng!"

"Funny you should mention that. Tseng said the same thing about you. Answer me this: Could you have diagnosed this patient as fast as Tseng did?"

"Tseng is arrogant, incapable of having a bedside manner, and he's clearly a mind-addled drug addict!" The words come out like punches. The fighter is back in the ring. But the woman doesn't match his energy.

"And you, my friend, are narcissistic and arrogant as well," she replies, "but with a wonderful bedside manner that, though no doubt very comforting, couldn't quite come to the correct diagnosis, could it? While I agree that a patient should feel that a doctor genuinely cares about them, at the end of the day, feelings don't cure patients; medicine does."

A long pause follows. He considers another retort. But every good fighter knows when he is beaten. With a sigh, he says, "You promised me a new identity. What name should I use to sign?" "That's up to you."

"How about Chris?"

"Chris." The woman pauses. "Yes, that works." She continues. "Chris Goodman. Because I believe you are a good man."

Chris pauses briefly, then gives a smile, but not a wide one. A smile of hope, a renewed belief that his life would finally matter again. He signs his new name with a flourish. "So," he says, "Prague, huh? How's the vodka here?"

# CHAPTER V

# DOCTOR DELIVERANCE

RONALD IS HUNCHED OVER HIS laboratory, pressing freshly made powder into pristine white pills. They look as professional as anything you'd find in your local pharmacy. They won't get you high, but this operation is strictly illegal. That's why this expensive equipment is hidden out of sight, in the basement of an ordinary, aging suburban Californian home.

Among the harsh chemical smells, Ron suddenly notices something unusual. Smoke. He sniffs the air, and looks around for evidence of a fire. But the Bunsen burner is out. He hears a scream from upstairs.

"Mom!" he yells, flinging open the basement door and sprinting up into the house.

The living room is already black with smoke, which is spreading along the walls. His mom is standing there in a panic.

"Ron!" she screams.

"Those bastards," Ron mutters to himself as he sprints toward her. They can feel the brutal heat scorching their skin. Breathing is hard, and they both start to cough. A wall of flame blocks the front door. Ron grabs his mother, and jumps with her out the window. They stumble and fall into the pool in their backyard. Catching their breath, they turn around and see their whole house up in flames as Ron's chemicals in the basement feed fuel to the fire that probably could have otherwise been put out by.

"I'm so sorry, Mom," Ron says. "This is all my fault."

The waitress coughs as she hands a cup of coffee to a thin African American man sitting at a round table. Ronald shoots the server a nervous glance, before accepting the coffee with a polite "thank you."

Ronald sips his coffee wearily as he sits facing the door of the truckstop diner. An alarm goes off on his watch. He takes a white bottle out of his satchel, and carefully extracts a selection of pills. "Cocktail hour," he mutters to himself, an ironic smile flitting across his face. He looks older than his 30 years. A deep, red gash runs down his cheek. Both his arms are wrapped in clean, white bandages.

A ginger-haired man walks in and looks around anxiously, before spotting Ronald hunched over his coffee. He notices the pill bottle still on the table. "Started without me, Ron?" he says with a wink. Then the smile falls from his face as he notices Ron's injuries. "Dude, what happened to you?"

"It's nothing," Ron replies, forcing a sad smile that crinkles his eyes. "Just an extra precaution. That's also why we are meeting here and not our usual spot. How are you feeling, Ned?"

"Good!" Ned's smile is genuine, trusting. "CD4 count at 500. Today is a good day."

Ron's smile vanishes. "I'm glad you're well, Ned. But I'm sorry, today is not a good day." Ron takes another white pill bottle and hands it to Ned, saying, "This is the last batch I'm going to be able to get you for some time. Someone burned my mum's place down on Monday. That's how I got hurt. We only just made it out alive. The police suspect arson, but they don't know who."

Ned looks shocked, but the concern in his eyes is for Ron, not himself. "Must be big pharma!" he cries. "Those bastards have been after you for years. But we'll be okay, man. There's always a way. We won't forget what you've done for us. Especially what you've done for me."

"Hey faggots," a harsh voice yells out across the din of the truckstop diner. The chatter of the other customers goes quiet as three large white men armed with bats swagger into the grimy cafe. "Oi fags!" yells the one in front, a monstrously tall man in a black leather jacket, skinhead bald with a swastika tattooed on his forehead.

The other customers stare into their coffees, avoiding eye contact. They could call the police. They could intervene. But even the bulkiest, bearded truckers shuffle nervously in their seats, trying to read their fortunes in the dregs of their drinks. The thugs know that they can go about their business unimpeded here. This is a place where people come in order to leave. They have schedules to keep, loved ones to return to, and thousands of miles of highway to go. One thin, black stranger ain't worth dying for.

Ron, knowing his days are numbered anyway, looks up at the thugs calmly. Ned grips his pill bottle tightly. "Got your medicine, fags?" taunts the bald man. "Better hang on tight to that. I hear something bad mighta happened to mommie's laboratory." The three thugs cackle.

"Ned, I think we should be leaving," says Ron, his voice still steady.

"Not so fast," the bald man says, leaning down and putting his face right next to Ron's. He hisses, "See those two handsome fellas there?" He gestures to his comrades, both dressed in black leather with their motorcycle gang logo stitched on the back, looking murderous. "Well, they're armed. Me, I don't care for guns. Far too clean. But Bobby over there is one of the best shots in the city. And if you're as smart as the boss thinks you are, you'll come with us without any screaming. Alright?"

Ned has gone a whiter shade of pale, but Ron just nods and stands up with defiance and a sense of bravery you wouldn't expect from a chemist. "Ned stays. He's got nothing to do with this."

The three huge thugs and the thin doctor walk out of the diner together. Ron feels a jab in the back, which he knows to be the cold steel of a handgun. "Keep walking. Don't make a sound. Oi!"

Once outside, the leader of the gang asks for Ron's car keys. Ron hands him the key with a smile.

"What are you smiling at, you fag?"

With a punch to the gut, Ron is on his knees. The sweet chirp of the remote unlock feature of the car is heard, followed by the even sweeter sound of a chemical explosion as the car detonates, right on queue. Ron, not being a big guy, moves fast, grabbing the baseball bat from one of his stunned assailants and using it in a desperate fury to whack away his assailants.

Trusty Ned, always thinking one step ahead, pulls up in his car and yells at Ron to get in. They screech away, making sure to run over and knock down the motorcycles as they leave.

"Where to, Ron?" says Ned.

"Barstow-Daggett Airport," Ron replies."Got a friend named Mike who works on the Black Hawk helicopters there. He will give us a lift to safety."

The hangar is empty. Ron calls out to Mike, but there is no response. A tall, confident woman strides toward him from behind what appears to be a small Learjet. "Ronald Meyers, I presume," she says, proffering her hand in greeting. "My, my, my, you handled yourself quite nicely at that truck stop. Now, my methods are certainly more subtle than those gentlemen—but I am still going to have to insist that you accompany me."

Ron turns to Ned. "Get out of here. You've done enough for me, but it looks like it is the end of the road for me." Ned, in tears, quickly hugs Ron, runs back to his car and drives off into the night.

The woman leads Ron to a large, dark van parked outside the jet. The woman follows him in, and slams the door shut. The vehicle speeds away, only to stop in front of a large commercial aircraft.

The white interrogation room. Big table. Bright lights. Yep, you're familiar with this place. Liz and Chris were here first. Ron was nervously waiting outside. But Liz and Chris aren't the names their parents gave them. So forget "Ron." He'll have a new name soon, too.

The last man is led into the room. The woman who grabbed him outside the cafe is waiting there. As always, she looks calm and in control.

"Most people who are here made many mistakes," the woman says, looking down at the thin man, "but you made only one. You got AIDS and were shunned by your peers at the clinic and forced out of your career by your superiors. But instead of letting your diagnosis destroy you, it drove you to help others. You set up an illegal pill-manufacturing center in the basement of your mother's house. You helped those who were poor or without insurance get access to the medicine that kept them alive. But you made some powerful enemies."

Looking the woman in the eyes, the thin man asks calmly, "Was it you?"

"No," she says. "Forgive me, I should introduce myself. I am Agent Thompson. You can address me as Tiffany.

We aren't here to harm you. In fact, we heard about what was going to happen too late to save your home, or your lab." "So why am I here?"

"You want to help others. But now you're powerless. We're here to help you contribute more."

"I'm a gay, black man with AIDS. I have no more gifts left to give."

"If we were still in America, maybe you'd be right. But we're not. Through us, you can do great things. We'll give you and the people you cared for access to the best medicine—pills that aren't even on the market yet. We can restore your medical license. We can give you the power to save thousands of lives."

Ron stares into space for a moment. "My mom," he says. "Can you protect her?"

"With you out of business, presumed dead, you will no longer be a threat. They'll leave her alone. And we'll keep an eye on her just in case."

"Okay. I'm going to need a lab to continue my research, as well as access to chemical agents that will be hard to find. You could say I've been dying to get my hands on them. Is this something you can facilitate? In either case, it seems I have no choice but to trust you. You seem fully aware of this. And besides, my life expectancy without medication is very short."

"One last thing," he adds. "I am curious to know the reason Doctor Tseng takes medicine. Was the medicine MDMA?"

Tiffany is amused. "You are very perceptive. I suggest you ask Doctor Tseng yourself, as you will be working under him."

Smiling, the woman slides a contract over the table. "You're going to need a new name," she says. "Something that won't draw attention. How about … Gary Smith?" She lowers down and whispers into his ear, "A lab for you will not be a problem."

"I prefer Greg," the man answers. Taking a pen, he signs "Greg Smith" on the dotted line. He stands and warmly shakes the woman's hand.

# CHAPTER VI

# CZECH MATES

THE THREE DOCTORS LEAVE THE basement, I assume heading to separate interrogation rooms. The voice in the sky gave away too many hints, too many details about me. Only one person in my life could be behind this charade. Jeff. The shadow that never leaves you. The devil behind his angelic looks and demeanor. Finally, he reveals himself for what he truly is: a wolf in sheep's clothing.

The big brother trying to ruin my life again. I looked up to him. He was the talented one; I was the smart one. He is charming; I am surprised he is not married—probably his occupation. I always had my suspicions that he was in the espionage game. But he is kind, too kind for that line of work.

Years ago, he would travel all over Europe. He called it backpacking. I, on the other hand, stayed in Prague to study medicine. But growing up in the South, you learn things that other kids don't. He taught me how to shoot a shotgun, a rifle, and a recurve bow. He is older than me, and in many ways a father figure.

But the most revealing detail that gave him away was his knowledge of wushu—Chinese kung fu. We were walking back to my flat in Prague I think three years ago or maybe four, when two men pulled their knives on us. Let's just say he quickly disarmed both of them before taking out two karambit knives, spinning them at lightning speed and knocking them out without killing them. I think that is enough nostalgia for now.

Jeff walks in, smiling. I know the drill; he who speaks first loses. The power dynamics. That familiar feeling of comfort and anxiety, of competition and reluctant affection. He takes a seat in the empty wheelchair facing me.

"Two truths and a lie," he says in his Southern drawl. I guess he feels comfortable. I notice he sounds more country when he's had a bit too much to drink, or is around family.

The childish game of hearing three statements and finding or guessing which statement is a lie. I don't respond. I just let him talk. The more he talks, the more information I'll have to process. "You used to love this game when we were younger," he says. "I'll start. I am your adopted brother, your protector, and your savior."

The God complex—apparently I am not the only one with this disorder. Enough of this; he never shows his hand. I've played poker enough times with him to know this. Besides, I am angry now.

"Protector is the lie," I say. "You were never my protector. Where were you three years ago? As a protector, you've failed. You want to believe that, but I am sorry to break it to you; that is the lie."

Jeff's facial expression doesn't change. He always baits me to talk. He knows I am still angry at him. I tire of this childish game. My turn, I take the bait; I was always horrible at this game.

"I know you are a spy, I know I am back here in Prague, and I am tired of being your asset. Go find another patsy. You are the worst. Jeff, who is your boss? Who is he that commands you? I want to speak with him. I can't believe you drugged me—was it through Tiffany? Wow, I knew it was too good to be true. Why would anyone want to work for me, let alone a hot young blonde. Why fly me back to Prague? There is a reason I left Prague. I had a wonderful life in Prague and in a matter of minutes it was ruined. You've ruined my life enough and you owe me."

I am still very angry at him, but Jeff does have a heart. We are brothers after all. He replies to me with a hint of kindness.

"Hoss, patsy is the lie. You were never the patsy. You just got caught in the crossfire. I never used you, but I always told you be careful who you sleep with. The right woman can be your salvation and the wrong woman can be your destruction. I apologize for failing you as a protector, but I am here to save you, and be your brother again if you'll let me."

Typical of him to offer an apology that makes it sound like I should be thanking him.

"Alright savior, what do you want from me?"

Jeff was never one to waste words. "Why do you think I brought you here? I want you to work for … with me. For the CIA. I want you to be my colleague and not a pawn."

I laugh at him. I am the worst spy, and fair enough, movies are movies for a reason—James Bond, Jason Bourne, Jack Bauer, Jack Reacher, Jack Ryan, they don't exist … I am not even a Johnny English! But apparently just being me almost got me killed three years ago. Should I accept his offer, or leave through the door and disappear? I've done it once … I can do it again. He knows what I am thinking, and his patience runs out.

"Tseng, you can't hide forever. Let's finish what you accidentally started three years ago in Prague."

I know there is more, and frankly I can't remember what I started yesterday, let alone three years ago, so I keep quiet. Time for him to talk.

"Tseng, you don't have a choice. The field director likes you and is impressed with your performance today, but the director will not speak to you. You are already back in play. You are the bait and the only thing I can do is to protect you. So, as far as I am concerned, I am your protector."

Jim walks in. "Hi Tseng, did you miss me?"

Huh, he speaks to me as if we are old friends. Oh Tseng, just play along. Jeff, thinking he is funny and clever, says, "Tseng, meet your new Tiffany."

# CHAPTER VII

# COMING OUT

THEY HAD TO FIND OUT sooner or later. I just didn't want it to be like this. I'm sitting down in the office—not alone, as Johnnie Black and I are having a splendid conversation, and then these three "doctors" come in and start pestering me. Do they want medical advice? Do they want to test my deductive powers? No, they want to get me, who is never sober, drunk. Or at least more drunk than I already am currently as I pound the shot of whiskey in my hand.

Now, normally I'm all for this. A double whiskey on the rocks, please. But the catch is, they want to get me drunk outside, in Prague, among people. Prague's fine. I have a lot of memories from this place … I think. Oh, I could tell you stories. Perhaps I will, if you're good. But it's the people part that bug me. Oh, and they want to be those people. With me. In town. Socializing. No. Thank. You. Too bad I can't tell them that; I apparently have a target on my head, they might not want to be with me and get caught in the crossfire. I am a spy now, so Jeff says, well more like bait, but either way, time to play it cool and not reveal too much.

"Come on, Tseng!" It's Liz this time. Pretty thing, but still … people! She doesn't even try to seduce me to convince me to go. I am still wondering whether the kiss from her was real or just in my imagination. It doesn't matter; I don't budge.

"Look," says Chris, "You're a rude bastard. But we have to work together now. So I'm gonna be the bigger man." He sticks out his hand to shake mine. I ignore it. This pisses him off. His face flushes.

"Look, Tseng," Greg this time, ever the peacemaker. "One drink in town, come on. What do you say?" Huh, if I knew any better, I'd say he was hitting on me. Funny I know, the unapologetic arrogance in me. Women want to be with me, and men want to be me and apparently, with me as well.

"I say, no!" The bottle flies out of my pocket and into my hands with incredible speed and grace. The lid pops open and a pill flies from bottle to hand to mouth in a matter of seconds. Good God, just kill me already! Where is that assassin when you need him?

"Yes, come on!" Chris again. "I know we got off on the wrong foot. But let's sort this out. I'll buy you the first round."

"Fine," I reply, "Double scotch on the rocks, please." I hold out my hand expectantly, but it is clear that whiskey is not forthcoming. Just more entreaties.

"Come on!" says Liz. "I'm too pretty to be stuck in the office all day." She winks at me. "Come on, Tseng. Show me how a real man parties."

"You're moving on to seduction now?" I say, "Well, warn me when it's Doctor Chris's turn so I can pretend

69

to be unconscious." "Look, mate," says Chris, putting his flushed, angry face right into mine. "We're gonna be stuck here, working with each other, for a long time. You have nothing else to do, so get off your ass and come with us for a goddamn drink!" "Piss off."

A mild rebuke, you would think, right? But not for Doctor Chris. Oh no. The big man snaps. Standing over my chair, he takes a swing. His fist collides with my cheek. I'm knocked off my chair, onto the floor. Without hesitation, Liz puts Chris in a headlock. She handles herself incredibly well against a larger, more powerful opponent, but Greg, predictably and weakly, steps in between me and Chris and grabs Chris by the shoulders.

"Oh, look who's off his chair. Well, you're gonna have to get up now, Tseng," Chris says, smirking over me.

Jeff walks into the office calmly as if he were the conductor of this orchestra, turns around and waves a beautiful redhead dressed in scrubs away as she approaches me with apparent concern. "So, the secret is out," he says.

Doctor Chris, who now appears to be frightened, looks over to Jeff. But the gorgeous redhead—there's something familiar about her. Or do I just have a thing for redheads wearing scrubs and glasses?

Jeff walks over to Chris and says in a hushed voice, "You punched my brother and he probably deserved it, but he is still my brother. Next time you are unable to control your anger, I will remind you who your superior is in every way. I will only say this once: you report to Tseng and Tseng reports to me. Keep your anger in check or there will be consequences."

Jeff walks over to me and helps me back into my chair. "What secret?" Liz asks, looking concerned now.

"I'm …" I look around. Am I embarrassed, ashamed, or just annoyed? Let's go with a cocktail of all three. I pop a pill and with a deep sigh, say, "I can't walk. I'm a paraplegic."

The three doctors look at each other, embarrassed. Doctor Chris's angry red face has turned pale. Doctor Greg was probably hoping I was gay and not a paraplegic. I must really fancy Doctor Liz if I care to know her reaction. Great! She takes pity on me. Just what I need—more people to pity me. If I wanted pity, I would have created an Instagram account and seen how many pity followers I could gain. Well, screw that sob story. I quickly pull out a flask from my pocket and take a big swig.

"I'm sorry," he says. "I didn't know."

"I have a wheelchair. It's in the cupboard." Greg turns around, and fetches it out.

"Electric! Nice ride," he says, trying to smile. Chris sticks out his hand. I stare at him for a moment, before taking it and struggle into the chair.

"Fine," I say, sitting in my motorized chair. "Let's go and have that drink. Pretty sure you can't be busted for drunk driving in this thing anyways and Doctor Chris, you owe me two drinks before I even contemplate forgiving you for the bruise on my face." Jeff looks amused as he and I both know I am the bait. Hopefully tonight is not my last night.

Ah, Prague. The glorious old town. Medieval spires, grey and gold, the portrait painters and living statues, bars lining the winding river, and the immortal grace of the Charles Bridge. And the beer. And the women. The memories are flooding back! As well as the sting of an old, repressed fear. Hmmm. That must mean too much thinking. So, speaking of flooding …

"Guys, this'll do," I say. We've been hiking (well, rolling, in my case) around the winding streets of the town center, and I spot a bar that looks vaguely familiar. Maybe I've been here before, or somewhere like it. Just classy enough that Doctor Liz won't feel out of place, just simple and local enough that we'll probably be the only Americans there. Perfect.

"Sit down, sit down," I say, motioning toward a cleanish table in the corner. The place is decorated like a grand old hotel, with portraits of serious, moustached men on the walls, a chandelier. But it's not too posh. You get the feeling that, though it's trying to be grand, this is a place where it is acceptable to get drunk. There is only one entrance and one exit. I am pretty sure I will see my angel of death before he sees me. In the meantime, I can wait for death with a drink in my hand.

I roll up to the bar, stretch up as high as I can in my chair, and rap my knuckles on the counter. Greg walks over and says, "Um, need some help there?"

"Relax, Mom," I say. "This isn't my first rodeo." The barman mumbles something in Czech and points to our table. I head back to our table with Greg, and a nice-looking waitress with the top half of her perfect tits sticking out of her uniform comes over and addresses Chris in Czech.

"Co piješ?" asks the bartender. He looks confused, stammering like a moron as he stares at her tits. I rap the table sternly, and say, "Prosim vas Pět piv a dvojitá whiskey s ledem."

The waitress makes five tallies on a paper with a P in front and two tallies with a W in front and leaves it on the table. I tell Doctor Chris, "Don't lose the tab," and point to the piece of paper. "I believe the first round is on you."

Chris looks stunned, and Liz shoots me a grin from the table in the corner. Five beers appear, plus my double whiskey.

"Um, Tseng, why'd you order six drinks?" says Greg, as Chris helps himself to his beer. "There's only five of us."

"For now," I say, "Na zdraví!"

We all clink glasses, but Greg is looking worried. "Oh relax," I whisper. "You have HIV, not cirrhosis. A drink won't hurt you. And I know that Jeff slipped you your medicine after Doctor Chris punched me, so you should be feeling fine." Speaking of medicine, time to get the party started. I pop another pill. The doors to the pub swing open. "Ah, speak of the devil."

Jim swaggers in—the tall, scary bloke whom Doctor Liz tried to cripple, who tried to stop Doctor Greg's house from getting burned down, and who escorted Doctor Chris away from an illegal cage match. He and I go way back, too … Wait! Do we go way back, or was that my sarcasm to hide my nervousness? But more on that later.

With Jim, I am sure Jeff has a reason to send him over to watch us. Usually to protect us, but can he protect us from ourselves or at least from a self-destructive me? Jeff follows Jim in and heads over to us. Jim stays by the door trying to blend in with a beer in his hand.

"One thing y'all seem to be forgetting," says Jeff, handing out 1000 koruna notes to each of us. "Drinks ain't free in this country. So y'all be needing an advance on your salary."

"Drinks aren't free, huh?" says Liz. "Wanna bet?" She downs her pilsner with one flick of the wrist, undoes the top button on her tight blouse, and heads into the increasingly crowded lounge.

"Someone's drinking for free tonight," says Chris, pocketing his 1000 koruna note and heading toward the bar, "but it ain't gonna be her. Wish me luck!"

Greg turns toward me, a sympathetic smile on his face. We know he isn't going anywhere, and perhaps he expects the paraplegic will stay with him in the corner, looking sad. Dream on, pal. My legs may not work, but I'm still a man from the waist down. And anyway, what's the point in learning this tongue-twisting language if I never get the chance to use it? Grabbing the spare beer I bought for this purpose, I roll out into the bar.

I'm six or seven drinks deep. Six or seven doubles. So that's like … 12 or 14 drinks … 13 on average, which is an unlucky number. Hmmm. Better have another one, just to be safe. Doctor Chris is over there, trying to flirt. He thinks that if he just keeps acting as American as possible, all the panties are gonna magically drop. The fool. It doesn't work like that. Well, not anymore, sadly. No, these days you need to actually take an interest in the girl.

Chris slinks away after another rejection, and goes to join the others at the table. Liz has probably broken a few hearts and is looking tipsy. She's sipping from an elaborate pink cocktail that some poor sucker bought for her. Greg is still on his second beer. Jeff is drinking red wine, and pontificating about something boring to Greg. Too bad Jeff isn't Doctor Greg's type; they look cute together. Jim is still in the corner drinking his non-alcoholic beer. The others keep shooting glances toward me though. Well, if you're gonna watch, you might as well learn.

I pop a pain pill, and chase it down with a slug of whiskey. I notice a girl, cute, redhead, fiery, watching me over her champagne. Ahh, there's something about redheads that drives me even crazier than the blondes do! Doctor Chris was hitting on her before, and now she's getting her ear chewed off by some Czech hipster with an eyebrow piercing. Something isn't right though.

I roll up to the team, finish my whiskey, and slap the empty glass down onto the table. "Dr. Tseng," says Liz, grinning, "we were just wondering how you …"

"Vacation's over, folks," I say, cutting her off. "I just found our next patient."

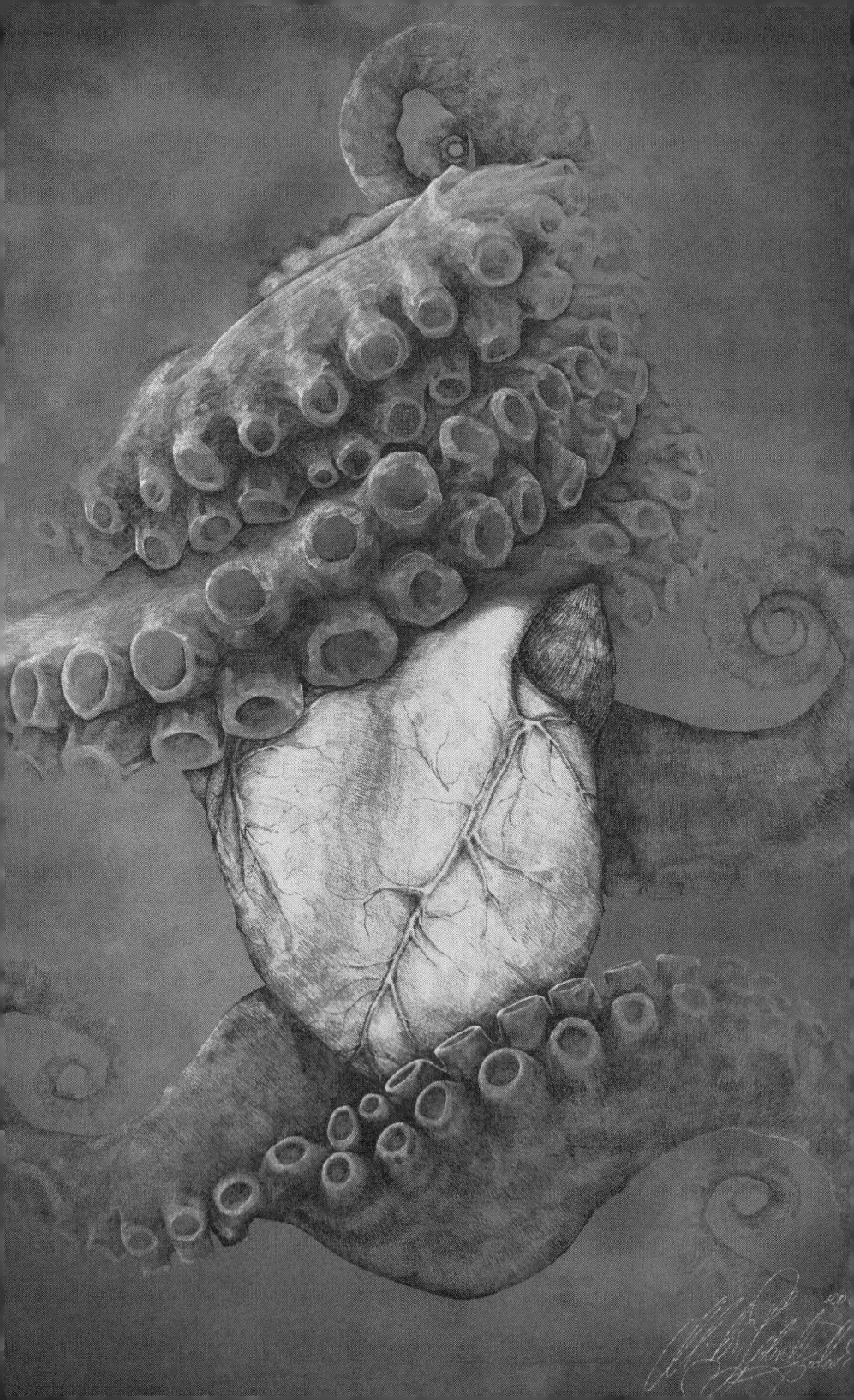

# CHAPTER VIII

# Heart

IT'S GETTING LOUD. LIKE A rehearsed performance, everyone in the bar seems to be raising their voice in uniform. The building is still classy, but the atmosphere is increasingly less so. You have to shout to be heard over the racket and din.

The others are still sitting down. I've seen the woman—the shapely redhead whom Doctor Chris was trying to hit on before. She watches me as the boring hipster talks her ear off in Czech. But I ignore her. First to be served at the bar. A wheelchair helps. Use the whiskey to wash down another pill. I'm drunk but not too drunk to think. This woman is unwell. But I can't go and talk to her. Too obvious. That's Doctor Chris's style.

No. Time to play this game properly. Like chess. My next move … There! I spot a group of three dark-haired girls sitting in the corner, looking bored. I roll up to them (that sounds a bit gangster).

In drunken Czech, I say "Ahoj studenti. Kdo čtete ve třídě?" They look up, surprised.

"I heard you talking to your friends," says the leader of the group in English. "You're American. But you speak Czech!"

"Yes, I do, but what you really want to ask is …"

"How does a creepy guy know that we're studying literature?" Oh, they just called me creepy. Tseng, you really are losing your touch and your age is beginning to show—but I know the game better than most, so time to reply in kind.

"Ouch, don't confuse me with one of your pathetic professors. The three of you are really quite obvious."

"We're obvious?"

"Yes. Look. Expensive shoes, but old. Assuming you are students, you probably haven't been earning a lot recently. That, plus your age and clothing style are typical of students. You all have oversized handbags with you. That equals books or a tablet for reading. And your fashion sense says arts, not science. Too relaxed, too conscious, too … messy."

"Messy?" They're starting to look pissed off, but intrigued. Anyway, I only need them for another moment. And no one is going to slap a man in a wheelchair! Come on.

"It's a compliment. Plus, I overheard you tell your friends this is the bar Hemingway goes to. Or I suppose I should say went to. He must be over a hundred by now, right?"

I notice out of the corner of my eye that the redhead is glancing my way, but keeps forcing herself to look back to the man sitting beside her. He goes to the bathroom, giving her a slap on the behind as he leaves. Now is the time.

"Okay, ladies, happy reading!" I turn and roll, pretending to head back toward my friends. But I know I won't make it. As expected, I feel a hand on my shoulder, and look up into a beautiful, blue-eyed face and a sea of red hair locks.

Evelina, the redhead from the bar, has joined us at our table. Chris is acting eager, preening himself. He still thinks he has a chance. The fool. But she has eyes only for me. Sensible girl. Doctor Liz looks annoyed. Good. I love playing games.

"You're big man with not so much smarts!" Evelina says to Chris, before turning back to me. "He approaches me, but you ignore me and talk to everyone else. Why I am not pretty for you?" "I wanted to give Doctor Chris here a chance. I hope you two will be happy together," I say, playing it cool. She rolls her eyes. Chris blushes.

"Let's play a game," I say. "I ask you yes-or-no questions and if you will answer all of them with yes, you buy me a beer … make that a shot of whiskey. If you answer no to one of my questions, I owe you a dinner and a movie."

"Okay … sounds interesting."

"You're Czech, but not from Prague … Brno? You work as a model, and you're … 23. No, 24."

"Wow. Very good, Mister."

"Just Tseng," I reply. "But now I'm bored. Good luck with your games."

She gets up to leave, but I gently take her by the arm. I know she wants to stay.

"Okay, I am just getting warmed up. If you leave now, you will be disappointed and you would owe me a drink. You have no brothers but one younger sister. You've recently been to Brazil. You were competing in a beauty pageant but you did not represent the Czech Republic. You represented another country ... Colombia."

She's looking surprised now. Maybe a little freaked out. But certainly impressed. I'll take it. Her accent was strong Slavic with a hint of Spanish, tan lines on her feet caused by Brazilian Havaianas, the light lingering smell of spray tan, the flawless hair extensions easily unnoticed by everyone except me and probably Doctor Greg, and finally the dead giveaway of a bracelet made of black onyx stones with one glass circular bead in the colors of the Colombian flag.

"Your mother is Colombian and your father is Czech. You recently went to the doctor complaining about chest pain, and had an EKG done to rule out a heart attack. It wasn't a panic attack either. You've been seriously ill. Let's ask my colleagues. What do you guys think?"

"Who are you? Am I being pranked? Are you really a doctor?" she asks, clearly shocked but also intrigued. I reply, "I actually am not a doctor, but I do teach medicine."

"How do you teach medicine without being a doctor?" she asks as she looks around for hidden cameras.

"Simple. Let me show you." Silence.

"Come on, people. Diagnose!" I say, with drunken verve. Greg speaks first, "Give her heparin stat … Okay, maybe not a good idea to be diagnosing when I am tipsy, but in all seriousness she might need warfarin to prevent another clot."

I turn to Evelina and say, "Don't mind him. He is truly on the right track even if he is wrong."

Greg, of course, continues to talk. "Seriously, I think it is deep vein thrombosis that got lodged in the heart."

"Doctor Greg, ever the pharmacist, going for the travel and immobility due to a plane trip, but forgetting our patient is in her twenties and unlikely to be having clots in her legs," I say. "Nevertheless, you assume she is on the pill and a smoker, but nice try. I always like your diagnoses, even when they are wrong."

Doctor Chris's turn: "Heartburn. I mean, gastro-esophageal reflux disease."

"GERD?" I say. "Still trying to impress the pretty lady? So much potential and yet you still come up short for a big man. Okay, it wasn't a bad diagnosis, but still wrong."

I glance toward Liz, and then at Evelina.

I expect a lot from Doctor Liz. I mean, she did kiss me and I feel that there might be a bit of mutual attraction, or at least respect. She replies with Chagas disease—a deft diagnosis. But is it really that good, or am I just into her? It does tick all the boxes: Brazil … heart issues … and a bite wound from a bug could be easily hidden under all that makeup. How do I play this? Tell Doctor Liz she is wrong and embarrass her in front of Evelina, or praise her for a good guess which will probably sound condescending. Either way, she'll get pissed off.

"Doctor Liz, I like you the most, so I will give you a hint," I say. "Evelina, you are newly single. Your eyes are that of a huntress looking for fresh meat. You have a look as if you were in love but were betrayed. It happened about two weeks ago while you were away at the beauty pageant, and you found out. He slept with someone, someone close to you, so the pain is doubled. A friend? No, someone closer, your best friend. No, it must be your sister!" Evelina is quiet and with a stunned look, starts to walk away and leave as her darkest, deepest secret was just revealed to four strangers. Liz is looking thoughtful. She says, "Takotsubo cardiomyopathy!"

"Correct!" I turn to Evelina and grab her hand. "Basically, you have a broken heart. But there's good news. I think I have the cure." I take her hand and guide it to the back of my wheelchair, and together we head toward the bar.

# CHAPTER IX

# FIGHT OR FLIGHT

IT HAPPENED QUICKLY. A KNOCK to the head—unfortunately, my head. How did I get punched twice in one night? Why does everyone think they can just punch me? I know many times I deserve it, but I've had a bit to drink and am not sure who I pissed off this time. Dazed, I look up and see my assailant. Evelina quickly tries to stop him from a second blow that will surely put me out for good.

Thoughts race through my mind as I try to figure out if this is my assassin—but why would he punch me and not put a bullet in my head? More importantly, why would Evelina, a girl I barely know, defend me? Jeff and Jim are quick to react. Jeff is always my nanny in situations like this. He and Jim have been lost in their own world, but are, as always, quick to react to the danger. In no time, Jim restrains my assailant and Jeff quickly returns the favor with a strong punch to the face. Of course, it's the bloke who was hitting on Evelina earlier. But still, who punches a guy in a wheelchair?!

Unfortunately, it doesn't end there. The bouncer (I assume) quickly comes over and gives Jeff a bear hug. Poor sap, Jeff immediately responds; a quick head butt backwards breaks his nose, a backwards step quicker than lightning knocks him off balance and he is on the floor with the dead weight of Jeff on top of him. Jim knows he must move fast. His hands quickly uncurl a length of twine, binding the first assailant's hands behind his back. He knows he is still dangerous as he still has use of his legs, but surprisingly Liz is already on it. A couple of swipes to the back of the knee and the first assailant is down, unable to get back up. Jim looks at Liz with admiration or lust. But it doesn't matter; the bar is now lively with fights erupting everywhere.

Chris is alive now. Finally a way to channel his anger. He was always the strong one so he starts punching, kicking, doing what he does best—taking down opponents, but with a sense of respect as he remembers he is a murderer and he does not want to repeat what happened at the cage fight. Greg stays put in the corner, still nursing his drink. He is not scared. Not engaged. He just sits there, nonchalantly sipping his beer. Should I be impressed, or scared? A beer flies toward me, snapping me back to the present.

Jeff is finally free. The bouncer is up and trying to do damage control, not paying attention to the person who broke his nose. Jeff walks over to me and smiles—a relief, as I know this is not about me. He goes over to Liz and seductively takes off her scarf as she gives him a kiss on the cheek. Should I be jealous or should I be worried for Jeff? I am confused, but the momentum quickens as he grabs my wheelchair and starts using me as a weapon. Apparently an invalid man in a wheelchair makes for a good battering ram.

We plow through the masses and knock over three bar brawlers. Bad mistake, as now they turn their attention to us. I am not surprised; Jeff can handle himself and I know he would never put me into harm's way. But, unfortunately you can never underestimate your opponent. One of the men pulls a knife. As expected, Jeff is prepared. The scarf moves fast, guided by the hands of a Jedi master who for years must have trained for a situation like this. The scarf wraps around the hand of the assailant and with a quick twist is brought to his back. A light kick to the back of the knee and the assailant collapses. Jim is quick to seize on the opportunity with his handcuffs and one down, two more to go. Who is this Jim with handcuffs ready at his disposal? Seriously, who brings handcuffs to a bar?

Jim handcuffs the first of three, but takes a punch to the head. No worries; Tseng to the rescue. I roll over and ask the second man something silly to throw him off. I ask him if he has a babcia—grandma. Jeff grabs my chair and quickly pulls out an umbrella from the chair. "Here, use this," he says. I don't argue. I revel in the moment of feeling alive as I thrust and slash my opponents with the umbrella.

The fight ends as quickly as it starts. The Czech police show up, but Jeff handles it. A thousand koruna bill is handed to one of the police officers and it's sorted. All the assailants and drunken attackers are removed into a van and escorted away from the pub. Jeff, a class act, returns the scarf to Liz and another thousand koruna bill is given to what appears to be the pub owner. Jim is stitching up Chris who has a deep gash on his arm from being cut with a glass bottle. Huh, Jim the bodyguard and nurse? Wait, I remember Jim; he was a medic with me and Jeff in the army. More importantly, come to think of it, Jeff is carrying a lot of thousand koruna bills. I probably should have him buy the next round.

I am stunned and silent. Also, should I be jealous? Doctor Liz is easy to read as she clearly is now very much interested in a wushu-fighting, charming, charismatic Jeff. But why do I even like her ... just because she kissed me? I am confused, but I don't care. Life is complicated. I take a pill as I am starting to feel the pain of being punched twice in one night. A shot of whiskey from Jeff and another one from Jim. "Na zdraví!" The three musketeers clink glasses and I black out as it doesn't matter anymore. I am just a pawn in this game called life.

"Have you told him?" Tiffany asks in a concerned voice.

The redhead stares at her coolly. The light shimmers, strangely, throwing focus onto her delicate features. Her mind is full of thoughts. Only a select few know who she really is—the field director of the CIA division in Prague. Few have ever held this position, and fewer still have survived till retirement.

"No and there is no need to. As far as I am concerned, he is a brilliant doctor." Her voice is musical. She continues, "Why do you care? It's not like he is your mark anymore. Besides, three years ago is a long time for anyone."

Tiffany knows her words are empty. Only she and Jeff know the truth. Although her subordinate, Tiffany warns her, "I know your time is limited, but act like an agent. Weakness will get you and Tseng killed."

Jeff storms in and Tiffany excuses herself. "I am pulling him from the field. Tseng is not ready. He swung that umbrella like a little girl. If you haven't noticed, he cannot walk or run away from danger, and I think Jim is tired of babysitting him."

The redhaired director takes a deep breath and responds: "The ninth inning! Three years we've been working on this mission, and three years we never got close to solving the riddle. He is your brother and he is our best hope at figuring this out, so stop bitching and act like an agent for your sake and for your brother's sake. Or maybe you would prefer to be reassigned?"

# CHAPTER X

# FRAGRANCE FROM THE PAST

THIS ISN'T THE FIRST TIME nor will it probably be the last time I've come to while lying on a hard floor. It's almost routine. The physical pain. The anxious faces. The flood of memories that charge back. Diagnosis: Shouldn't have had that 19th whiskey. Prognosis: a lot of stupid conversations, some medicine, and back to work.

"Your blood pressure is 90/40. You passed out," Chris says as a redhead in scrubs and glasses strides out of my office.

Wow, I like this hungover Chris! He is calm, polite, and even helpful. I look down and see that someone has changed my catheter and I have a new drainage bag. I look at Chris as if asking him if it was him that violated me while I was passed out. He smiles and tells me with a creepy wink that the redhead in scrubs took care of it. Anyways, joke's on them. Not the whiskey this time, suckers.

"It's low because of the opiates," I say. "Give me a cup of black coffee stat, and I'll be fine in no time. Oh, and Doctor Greg," I say as he turns to the coffee machine in the corner, "put a splash of whiskey in there." Chris offers me his hand and I scramble—with as much dignity as possible—back into the wheelchair.

"Who's the redhead?" Chris asks.

"I was about to ask you the same. She is hot."

"I think she is a nurse because she took your blood pressure as well as …" Chris again creepily looks at my crotch.

No sooner is the coffee in my hand when yet another strikingly beautiful woman walks into the room. She wears black stiletto heels, and is dressed in a vibrant red dress. Naturally, blonde hair. Makeup a little heavy, but my eyes don't linger long on the face. Hang on. Maybe they should. I know that face …

"Timothy!" she cries, looking at me, "Timothy? How are you?" She looks shocked, as if she's seen a ghost.

Have I been gone that long? Was that a question to me? Or was there something more?

"You should be dead!" Ouch. No one likes hearing an ex tell them this.

She continues: "I heard from the expat community a brilliant doctor was in town who could possibly help me." She clutches her head in a theatrical gesture of pain. "But I didn't know it was you! I cannot believe it. But I will be angry later. Now, you fix my head. Dead man."

"Um … good to see you too, Kristina." She deals a quick slap to my face, and I realize I should have just said, "Sorry."

"Good! Three years and not a word! You asshole!"

95

Kristina turns to Chris, who looks confused, and tells him, "Okay, you show me the examination room now. Two years I've had these pains. No doctor can fix it," she says in her thick but sexy accent.

"Doctor Chris, take her next door," I say, trying to summon a sense of control.

"No," she says. "I hate you. Why are you here? Where have you been? I don't want these peoples." She gestures dismissively at the room at large, and looks suspiciously at Greg, who calmly holds her gaze.

"These peoples work for … with me," I say, as steadily as I can. "I am the best, or was the best, at least in medical school. Did you forget those late nights you helped me study anatomy? These people are the next best. I'll keep an eye on them. Don't worry. Now …" I take a sip of my coffee and, knowing Chris is enjoying every minute of this painful reunion, I choose politeness to coerce him to get her away from me and into an examination room.

"Doctor Chris, please escort her next door to the examination room," I say.

Oh, the grin on his face seared into my mind. Chris, enjoy the moment, just enjoy it while you can. I pop two more pills into my mouth.

Greg and Chris have been watching this scene with a mixture of astonishment and amusement. Liz, however, looks a little stern.

"And who is she, Timothy?"

"Tseng," I correct her. "And she's somebody that I used to know. We met here many years back, when I was a student."

"Met where, in class?"

"Haha, no. Klub Nebe. Do you know it? We really ought to go there together sometime. It was easy. Just like the bar last night. I watched. I observed. And within a few minutes, I knew more about her than her closest friends. She seemed rather impressed by this, and, well …" I wink. "Ask Evelina," I say, a little smugly, referring to the redhead from the bar last night.

"Our Tseng likes strong women more than he likes strong whiskey," says Liz, rolling her eyes. Jeff walks in, and the others turn to him. "Do you know," asks Liz, by way of a greeting, "that Tseng, I mean Timothy Tseng, has a long-lost lover called Kristina?"

Jeff looks surprised for a moment, but quickly regains his stride. "Tseng doesn't go by that name anymore. And yes, I know Kristina; she and I have a history as well. But she's not as sweet as she seems."

Liz scoffs at this. "Sweet! Hmph! And do brothers share everything?"

Jeff, never one to feel uncomfortable, starts to clear his throat and regain his professional composure. "She's an ex-spy from Russia," says Jeff. "Keep an eye on her. We arranged for her to be checked by our doctors here. Tseng, I assume you can play the role of Timothy again for our sake, as we need information from her." "I think Doctor Chris might get jealous, but I will do as you wish, brother." Jeff doesn't miss my use of brother. "You know," I continue, "replacing my pills with a placebo isn't helping anyone." Jeff holds his stare, but I see genuine concern in his eyes. Oh, how I hate those puppy-dog eyes! He pulls out what I assume is a medical patch and as he sticks it on my upper middle back, he whispers to me, "I know you are speedballing." Within seconds, the pain subsides and he walks away.

With a clear mind, I turn back to my team, who are sitting in awkward silence. "The migraines are real, folks. So let's cure her. It's our job, right? So, team. What causes migraines?"

"Nothing causes migraines," says Greg. Oh Doctor Greg, if only you were a real woman, you would know most migraines only affect the fairer sex. But, if I go down that road, I won't be able to ask him for a favor I need from him. Better I just play it safe with a bit of sarcasm.

"Spoken like a true WebMD doctor. Anyone else?"

"Tumors, neuropeptide imbalance, trigeminal nerve irritation," says Chris.

"Run an MRI to rule out tumors. Run labs and examine her trigeminal nerve," I say. They all leave dutifully. I lean back in my chair and gingerly touch my sore cheek. Now where's that whiskey …

After some hours, Greg returns.
"Any news?"
"She kicked me out!"
"What?"

"She wouldn't let me examine her."

"Because you're gay?"

"Because I'm black, Tseng."

"Ah yes. Kristina is smart but not … enlightened. Ignore her."

"I am."

"And the results?"

"No tumors," says Liz, "Doctor Chris was able to evaluate the trigeminal nerve which looks fine. Doctor Chris is still in there with her, prepping the MRI."

"Okay, kids, time to let the adults show you how it's done. Get the door."

I roll into the room. I notice a sweet scent in the air. For most people, this would be a background detail. But when you have trained your faculties as I have, a simple scent can speak volumes. I head over to Kristina before I stop. There's something else that's been bothering me. It only takes one person to report back to me. Why did both Doctor Greg and Doctor Liz come back to give me this latest, trivial update? Time for that later. I sniff and lean in toward Kristina. But before I can speak, she leans in and whispers in my ear, "We need to talk alone."

"There's no need," I whisper back. "My colleagues here know how to keep a secret."

Kristina, not one to take no for an answer, proceeds to strip down, revealing all her curves to us and apparently a hidden knife in her garter. Doctor Chris stares and Doctor Liz rolls her eyes as she grabs Chris by the back of his white coat and drags him out of the room. Doctor Greg maintains eye contact with Kristina as he follows them out, leaving her and me alone.

"Are you going to continue staring at me or are you going to hand me my patient gown?" she says. I hand her her gown and remind her that the knife is made of metal and would not be allowed into the MRI machine. But wait, there is no need for an MRI; that scent ...

"New perfume?" I ask.

"I always wear this."

"No, no, no, Kristina, you didn't wear this scent when we dated. You wore Elie Saab with mandarin, orange, and jasmine notes. Your scent was like a summer breeze in Lebanon, but you knew that and you used that to seduce me. I was fond of you then and, to be honest, I am still quite fond of you, but things got complicated and it doesn't matter now, because," I sniff the air dramatically, "it smells like you have a new boyfriend."

"Timothy, you left me without a word, without an explanation," she says. "If you wanted to break up with me, you didn't have to fake your own death and yet, here you are turning it around, making me feel bad about having a new boyfriend. Look, we both moved on. You have the blonde doctor who likes you and feels threatened by me. I already know you've diagnosed me so just get to it and let's move on with our lives."

"Fine, give me the perfume bottle." "Why?"

"Just do it. Unless you want to keep having migraines."

She hands over a small pink bottle. A whisper from her into my ears: "Stop playing games. I know who you are and you should not have come back here, Tseng." I ignore her, calling her bluff. A quick look at the bottle and immediately I notice it is an unrecognizable brand, but I already know more than she thinks.

I look her in the eyes, looking for a tell. She smiles seductively at me. Looks like her migraine is gone … or was she faking it? A memory floods in. We are in Prague, in my old flat. She shows me something, asks me how my Chinese is. Of course I'd cleverly replied, "Not as good as my knowledge of female anatomy." Looking back, I cannot believe that line worked.

Liz, looking through the window of the control room, is getting impatient with my staring at Kristina's beautiful ruby lips. She comes back in and snaps her fingers in front of me, bringing me back to the present.

I smell the bottle like a dog onto the scent, and smile my egotistical smile before announcing my deductions. "Strawberry scented. Too bad, Kristina. You always hated strawberries. You really must like this bloke. Doctor Liz, what was her blood pressure?"

"Normal—120 over 80."

I take the cap off the perfume bottle and spray Kristina in the face.

"And now?" Kristina begins to feel light-headed and stumbles, barely catching herself on the examination bed.

Liz quickly takes her blood pressure. "90 over 50," she says, looking alarmed.

"Perfect. Pump her up with antihistamines and give her a little adrenaline and she should be fine." I turn to Kristina. "Congratulations, you are allergic to your new boyfriend, I mean allergic to strawberries. Most people who avoid certain foods are probably intolerant of them and over time may develop an allergy to them. Your new allergies caused a massive histamine release, lowering your blood pressure which caused your migraines. Talk about a toxic relationship!"

I leave, taking the perfume bottle with me. Jeff stops me in the office. "You were supposed to diagnose her, get close to her again, and subtly gather information, not piss her off. You do know who she is! You don't want her as an enemy!"

"Jeff, I was not born yesterday. I am pretty sure word of my return to Prague will get out through her." I throw the perfume bottle at him. "Look on the back," I say. "Made in Odessa. We're on her scent now. In Odessa you will find the answers you seek. In the meantime, I feel like the target on the back of my head just got larger thanks to you reconnecting me with Kristina."

"This can't end well." Jeff's voice is firm but not without respect. The redhead in the room ignores him. She walks over to her desk and sits down. She motions for Jeff to take a seat as she knows this will be a long conversation. She asks, "How many years have we worked together?"

Jeff replies, "Almost five years." The redhead adjusts herself in her seat. No point in hiding it anymore, she opens a desk drawer and takes out three bottles of pills. One by one, a pill from each bottle ends up in her mouth and down her throat. She pulls a bottle of whiskey and two glasses out of the bottom drawer. A tiny shot of whiskey into her glass and a full double shot into Jeff's. They say "Na zdraví" in unison as they clink their glasses.

"You follow orders and yet we all know you are selfish. We all are. He is your brother, he is your responsibility, and more importantly he is your asset. Use him and do what you were trained to do."

Jeff is soft. He knows the redhead knows his weakness, and it has always been his brother. Jeff is also not stupid. "I know you slept with him when he first arrived in Prague," he says. "I know you still care for him, but it doesn't matter now, does it?"

Her silence says it all.

Jeff, with genuine respect, tells her, "You are being reckless. You are going to die, and I know you want to die with honor, but don't get my brother killed." He gets up to leave, finishing his whiskey and leaving the empty glass on the desk.

# CHAPTER XI

# PORT OF NO RETURN

ER HIGH HEELS CRUNCHED SOFTLY on the ground, but the man didn't hear. His ears were muffled by a thick, woolen hat. Her training reminds her to kill or be killed. Ivan had confronted her for stalking him. Foolish man, he didn't feel a thing. The knife slid silently over his throat, and he crumpled onto the snow. If the dead man could talk, he'd tell you that the last thing he remembered was the faint smell of strawberries ...

These events happened before the story you're reading—but I found out about them much later. But you should know now. It will help you to understand the things I wrote as this was all happening. There is so much I should have remembered. So much that I hid. I hid from everyone, even from myself. Blame it on the pills. Blame it on arrogance. But in the end ... well, you'll find out soon.

It was the winter of 2016, on the northwestern shore of the Black Sea. Ukraine isn't famous for its weather. But Odessa is pretty mild. The exception is one week in February. The locals call it Hreschennya. During Hreschennya, things get bad. For Kristina, they got worse. Maybe she was in too deep. As I say, I only found out about all this much later.

The ships came in at night. The flags were innocuous enough: Baltic nations like Latvia and Estonia, mostly. And they contained legitimate goods. Refrigerators, and so on. But Kristina wasn't interested in that. If you knew the right people, had the right amount of foreign currency, could stand the pressure, you could get your hands on products that were far more exciting: cocaine from Colombia, guns from the factories outside of Moscow, Chinese white heroin.

On a particularly cold February night, Kristina was awaiting a special shipment. Something far more dangerous than what the professionally corrupt thugs who worked here were used to handling. Drugs destroy families. Guns can kill armies. But what Kristina was waiting for was on a whole other level of deadly. A few clicks using her iPhone 4, and she hurried away.

She saw the flag lit up by the floodlights of the port, and her heart jumped. She watched as the rusting ship glided softly toward land, looking so serene on the still water. But as she was watching the ship dock, someone was watching her. Kristina slipped down from the hilltop, and wandered down the street toward the noise and light of the port.

It didn't take long to find the man she was searching for. A heated exchange of Russian followed. She was led along the street, through a small alley, and through the back door of a large warehouse. Two guards shook her down, before a second steel door opened, and she entered what looked like a massive distribution center. An enormous floor, brightly lit, dozens of people in thick black jackets hurrying around, carrying cardboard boxes with Chinese characters on them. In other circumstances, it could have been the local Amazon warehouse. But she knew that there were no books inside those boxes. She quickly grabbed the bill of lading off an unoccupied desk.

While Kristina was in the factory, a man waited outside, hidden in a doorway in the small alley. He was relaxed. Although his home was far away, these streets were familiar to him. He had the advantage of knowing most of the key players. But few of them knew him. When he heard footsteps heading back toward the door, he flung aside his cigarette and disappeared.

As she furtively exited the factory, Kristina noticed the smell of tobacco, and saw the still-burning filterless cigarette slowly extinguishing itself on a dry patch of ground above a clump of snow. She knew she had been watched.

It was quick and fast. A knife to her throat, and a winter-gloved hand to her mouth. She didn't struggle. She knew that if she was meant to be killed, the knife would already have slit her throat. A faint whisper in her ear: "Killing Ivan was foolish, now you must finish what he started. Secure the shipment. I'll be watching."

There was a night train leaving to Kiev. From there, she could take a train to Lviv, hire a car, and slip across the border in Poland. Prague wasn't much further. It was familiar. It felt safe. More importantly, a friend who could read Chinese was there.

# CHAPTER XII

# BREATHLESS

A LOT OF DOCTORS WILL TELL you never to trust patients. Patients will lie about how much they drink, about how much they smoke, about the drugs they use, about being unfaithful to their wife. They're embarrassed, and they're stupid. But sometimes the truth you need to get at has nothing to do with their illness. Well, not really. This situation kind of only happens to doctors who have been kidnapped and taken to Eastern (okay, Central) Europe for clandestine reasons. And while today's case is very unusual for a standard American doctor, I get the feeling it's pretty typical of the kind of work we'll be doing here. Just two questions: Where did the director dig up this cadaverous man who is halfway to the grave ... and just who exactly is he?

We know him only as the Colonel. Once powerfully built, but now clearly ill. Faded. He has been out of the country for at least two years—don't ask me how I know this—and he refuses to tell me where. Very frustrating.

Also, he's dying. Which could be useful. Dead men don't tell tales. Dying men … well, let's find out.

I sit in my wheelchair in the examination room watching Doctor Liz deftly insert an IV catheter with great precision to a vein that's barely visible in the frail Colonel's arm. Why do I keep staring at her? The heart always wants what it cannot have and I am the epitome of that cliche.

Doctor Greg and Doctor Chris are working side by side. Greg examines the patient's eyes, nose, ears, and throat, while Doctor Chris sets up the oxygen tank and fixes a ventilator mask to the Colonel's mouth. I on the other hand am simply enjoying the moment as my minions do their doctorish things. But I can't get my mind off what I've just seen.

Before the Colonel was wheeled into my examination room, I smelled something in the corridor leading to the office. A door I thought that was just used by the janitor for … janitorial staff (don't ask me) was ajar. And inside, I heard voices. I opened it. There were stairs. I couldn't go down for obvious reasons, but in the dim light below I saw Greg and Chris hunched over a Bunsen burner. It didn't take a genius to figure out what they were up to. As it happens, one was on hand. So I played it cool. I only yelled a little. And they don't appear to have minded. They're used to my antics by now, and didn't seem to be trying all that hard not to get caught. Doctor Greg and Chris are becoming quite chummy, and I wonder if that is a good thing. Why do I even care? I've got bigger problems to deal with! My mind moves back to the Colonel.

Focus. I wheel away and head to the office. There's a big screen on the wall now, which means I don't have to go in there and get my hands dirty. Also there's a cool microphone so I can make myself heard in the exam room whenever I need to. Gotta thank the unions for looking after a hardworking paraplegic!

"It's just the flu," whispers an obviously fatigued and sick patient, barely audible through his ventilator mask. "Why are you doing all this?"

"Your symptoms are more serious than you think," says Liz, taking control and extracting some blood. "They sent you to us for a reason, Colonel."

"Can you tell me where you are?" Chris asks the colonel. He shines a small flashlight in the colonel's eyes to check the response of his pupils. "Who is the current President of the United States?" "Forget that!" I snap through the microphone. "Where were you for the last two years?"

The colonel coughs. "That's classified." He turns to Liz. "Who is that?"

"Unfortunately for us," says Chris, "that's our boss."

"And fortunately for you," interjects Greg, "that's your doctor." "Seriously, do I need three doctors to tend to me?" says the Colonel. "I am sure you have better things to do than to treat the common flu."

"Colonel, I am the voice of God," I say. "Just give me a region or country you were last in. We are here to help you, but of course I am here to save you." I think to myself, I am getting the hang of using this microphone. I slap a fentanyl patch on my back as a form of self congratulation. It's tiring, playing God.

Liz turns to the others as they roll their eyes. And just like that, the colonel's situation starts to deteriorate.

"Heart rate is increasing," says Liz. "Tachycardia. O₂ stats are dropping. Dyspnea. We're going to have to intubate." She quickly moves to the drawers and pulls out the equipment for intubation. "No!" I shout through the speakers. The voice from the sky, I like this. It feels powerful.

Jeff barges in. "You want to know who wants you dead?" says Jeff, shouting at the rest of us "Just save the Colonel's life because the same people who want you dead imprisoned him and only just released him when he became ill and a ransom was paid."

"Tseng, he's suffocating. If we don't do this now, he'll die," says Liz, genuine concern in her voice.

I ignore Jeff and Liz. "Wait for it," I calmly reply as if I know something they don't know. Of course I know something they don't know. Jeff looks nervously on the monitor.

"For what?" Liz asks, almost ready to disobey me and intubate the patient.

The colonel has gone pale. His lips are starting to

turn blue. Death isn't far away, but there's another stop before there which will give us an advantage—a clue to this stubborn, silent man.

"That!" I say. I see the colonel begin to seize, his eyes rolling up, his body twisting and flailing wildly. I love being right all the time. It's got to be an infection, but we will see what the others have to say.

"Now, sedate him and stabilize the patient before intubating," I say. "Doctor Liz, I know you are a skilled surgeon and have quick, precise hands, but intubating him during a seizure could damage his vocal cords and his ability to talk might become useful if we are to save his life. Once he's stabilized, meet me in the office."

"What causes respiratory infection and seizures?" I ask. "Or, to put it simply, what respiratory infection causes seizures?"

"An asshole doctor who thinks he's God?" says Chris.

"Not helpful," I say. "Someone other than Doctor Chris, the incarnate John the Baptist?"

"Small-cell lung cancer." Of course Doctor Liz chooses cancer; what surgeon doesn't want it to be a tumor that can be removed surgically? But at least she is trying. Why didn't I think of that myself? Oh, because it is not cancer—it's an infection!

116

Okay, let's be polite to her. God has a soft spot for hot blondes who know medicine.

"Not likely," I say. "He's a military man and he's still well built. Cancer would have held him back years ago."

"So … ?"

"Pulmonary emboli," says Greg. "It fits. When Tseng started interrogating him, his blood pressure spiked, dislodging a clot that caused the crash."

I am trying to stay focused, but my mind keeps flashing back to Doctor Greg and Doctor Chris together in their "secret lab."

"Fine, it fits," I reluctantly say. "Still not a diagnosis, but administer heparin and find the clot or proof of a clot if it's still there. Better play it safe. God would hate for the colonel to have a stroke."

"Take out the tube, Doctor Liz. I need to hear him."

"The tube is there so he can breathe, Tseng," she says. "You may remember from medical school that breathing is an important part of a healthy lifestyle—unless you are God or were too busy chasing mysterious Russian women."

Ouch, that almost stung. Why bring that up? Is Doctor Liz mad at me or jealous? It doesn't matter; I may not even live to see tomorrow as a target is apparently still on my head.

Jeff is being clever, trying to flush out my assassin. Reestablishing my relationship with Kristina is definitely going to get me killed. News of my return is bound to get out rapidly as Prague is a small city of 1.1 million people, and its expat community even smaller. Anyway, that's a mystery for tomorrow to solve. I slap a fentanyl patch on to help me focus.

"The only mystery that matters now is where this man has been for the last two to three years." I say.

"Who is he?" asks Greg. "Where has he been? That is the only way to narrow down the number of infections this could be."

"That's classified," I reply. This Colonel, whoever he is, has remarkable resilience to withstand pain and interrogation tactics. I have a feeling he could come in handy in helping me deal with my chronic pain. I whisper to myself, "Tseng stop giving yourself false hope" as I peel back another fentanyl patch and stick it onto my back.

Liz rolls her eyes and walks over to the camera. "Fine. I'll take out the tube. But try and be … human."

The Colonel looks at me coolly. The moment the tube is out, he starts wheezing and gasping for air.

"You were held captive," I say. "Marks on your wrists. Shows you were bound for a very long time. Kinky sex, maybe. But I think, in your case, there are darker forces at play than your ego. Tell me where you were held as a prisoner."

"That's classified."

"Well, that's a confirmation anyway. Now stop wasting my time."

"Tseng," says Chris sternly, who's been fretting beside an anxious Greg in the corner of the room. "He's not getting enough air. He's gonna crash again."

"Tell me!" I boom through the mic.

"Torture isn't going to work," pants the Colonel. "Whatever you can do, I've suffered worse. Death would be a relief."

"Fine, we will do this the hard way," I say. "Go x-ray his lungs and give me an MRI of his brain."

"The x-ray will be simple, but he will have to be still for the MRI of the brain," says Liz.

"Then do what they do with birds of prey and blindfold him so he stays frozen!" I say.

I roll myself back to my office and switch on the screen that now shows the MRI machine. The patient is rolled in and placed on the table. Good thing Doctor Chris is very strong. He easily moves the patient from his bed to the machine table. Dropping my voice low, I imitate Batman's harsh grunt, and say into the mic, "Do you know where you are?"

"Quit playing games, Tseng!" snaps Liz.

"MRI is starting—he needs to be still," says Greg. "And Tseng, that's the worst Batman voice I've ever heard."

"Look at his lung x-ray," says Liz, always trying to be proactive. "It's an infection. We just don't know what. Treat him with broad spectrum antibiotics."

I laugh villainously into the mic, and continue with my Batman impersonation—which is pretty good by the way; don't listen to Doctor Greg. "The mighty colonel has been struck down. We will try to cure you. Minions! Administer ribavirin!"

"Hep C? That doesn't affect the lungs!" says Liz.

"No," I say. "But Nipah virus does. This man has been held in a cave. And he has been infected by …"

"Bats!" the others chorus in unison.

"Dose him up and he'll be back to his old lying self in no time," I say. "But if he dies, then do an autopsy to confirm the diagnosis. Everyone here should take ribavirin as a precaution and we should be quarantined. Finally, I can get some sleep. Doctor Chris, call Jeff and tell him the good news: We are under self-quarantine for two weeks!" I pour a victory shot of 21-year-old scotch down my throat and pass out.

Jeff walks into the director's office. There is no need to knock; he is expected. A direct woman who likes discretion, the director would ordinarily have visited Jeff at his office. Something isn't right here. The woman is aware that her physical deterioration is showing. She hides in the shadow behind her desk. It's late and the only light is from the open door. She takes out a match and lights the three candles sitting on the table—a little trick she learned in the art of seduction, not that it matters at this moment. In this moment, what matters to her is to hide her illness and feel in control.

Jeff walks over and sits across from her. "How is the colonel?" asks the woman. Jeff replies that he is recovering, but can not speak still. The woman impatiently states, "Let me know the moment he is capable of a debriefing."

The candles reveal a decanter full of amber whiskey. Two crystal tumblers stand beside it.

"What are we drinking to?" he asks as he grabs the decanter and pours out two full measures. She takes the proffered glass and replies, "First to Tseng for saving the Colonel's life"—and with a flick of the wrist downs it in one go. "Second, well … it's my birthday."

She slides the glass back to Jeff for a refill and adds, "One year ago today I was told I would be dead in three months." Jeff stares at her for a moment, then hastily refills their glasses.

The silence is unbearable. But what should be said or could be said during a moment like this? The director tosses a file marked "For Destruction" to Jeff.

"You know we keep tabs on Kristina," she says. Jeff nods as he opens the file and looks at the contents under the flickering light of the candles. Old pictures spill out—photographs of Tseng and Kristina together at many locations.

"A Russian and an American in an unsanctioned CIA relationship," she says. "Plus security footage of Kristina whispering to Tseng multiple times in the examination room is damning evidence in itself." A screen is turned on showing video footage from the clinic. Kristina is seen multiple times whispering into Tseng's ears, but being a clever spy, she makes sure her lips are always hidden from view, preventing lip readers from deciphering her words.

Jeff remains cool and takes a swig from his glass. "What are you suggesting?" he asks.

"I don't suggest. I know," she says. "I know you were supposed to seduce her and turn her; she was supposed to be your mark, and you failed, allowing her to turn your brother into her mark." Jeff, following his training in resisting interrogation, gives nothing away. Then he decides to speak:

"We know Tseng is not a traitor, but he is the key to unlocking this mystery. You say you know; let's talk about what we know. The Russians were up to something three years ago and I believe that with the increased chatter, and because Tseng has resurfaced, they are now ready to make their move. I am pretty sure branding Tseng a traitor will not help you. There is a reason why you became director three years ago when Tseng disappeared from Prague, and after so many years without any major results, your frustration is going to jeopardize the mission."

"That will be all," she says calmly as she grabs Jeff's glass and refills it to the brim. "I always knew you were loyal, but as for your brother, I have my reservations. An unwitting accomplice is still an accomplice. If we find out that Tseng in any way helped the Russians knowingly or unknowingly, I will authorize his removal."

# CHAPTER XIII

# FEELINGS

"LET'S TALK ABOUT THE PATIENT, then," says Liz. I wake up in my chair, dazed and confused. Figure I'll pop a pill before opening my eyes. Huh, I've got my pills back, but where am I? Ah, the smell of beer. Ugh. Stale beer. I've been grumbling about spending time out of the office. Though in truth, I'm happy to be here in this bar. The whiskey is cheap and beer flows like water. But hang on …

"What patient?" I ask. "We don't have one! We are in quarantine if I remember correctly." I pop another pill and close my eyes. Oh, how I missed being in control of my pain management.

"Oh yes we do," she says and picks up a napkin off the wooden desk that is already damp with beer. It's only 3 pm and the small bar is already full. Out the window I see the sun dance across the cobbled streets of the old town. Liz holds the napkin up to her face as if it were an important, intricate document, and pretends to read: "Patient. 30-something male. Physically robust from the waist up. Experiences paralysis of the legs and frequent bouts of fainting. Also displays an affinity for mysterious women."

"Very clever," I say, taking a bottle of pills out of my pocket and waving it before popping two in my mouth and adding, "Not to mention chronic pain!" Lovely, I am back at the cafe but at least this time I am drinking beer. Although I hate beer. Tseng, don't overplay the fantasy.

"You're not in pain," says Liz. "It's in your head. Those pills are mints and I have your fentanyl patch."

"No," I say. "It's real. Now, excuse me." I am angry now and the cafe fades away. Now I am back in the bar. I don't complain; it's my dream. I look in my hands. Neat; it seems I am holding up a bottle of Johnnie Walker Black Label. "Me and my Johnnie need to spend some quality time together. She's getting lonely and yes, Johnnie is a she to me."

With a crash, the whiskey glass flies out of my hand, and the precious nectar spills across the sticky bar floor. Liz has leapt on me. She straddles me in my seat. She leans her face in close to mine, and whispers into my ear.

"Now Tseng," she sighs, almost moaning, "We're going to see just how hard you're going to be to figure out ..."

After a few (not unenjoyable) moments, Liz hops off and returns to her seat. Greg and Chris are staring with obvious astonishment. Doctor Chris looks angry. Jealousy? Who cares! I know he has a beef with me for being the alpha in our relationship.

"There," Liz says, looking satisfied. She takes up her napkin, and again pretends to read, saying, "Patient experiences paralysis of the legs only." She looks very pleased with herself as she takes the fentanyl patch from her bra, leans over with her tits in my face and reaches down the back of my shirt to place it on my back.

"So, Tseng," says Greg, who is less fascinated by this exercise than Chris or I. "What actually is wrong with you? There is something. All this fainting. You say it's the pills. But I don't think so. There's something there. And if we find out what it is, you may get better … if you want to."

I ignore him. Back to Doctor Chris. Something is missing. I stare at him. It wasn't anger; he truly was jealous, but not of me. Doctor Chris sees me trying to read him, and he takes control. "Tseng, give it a rest. You are trying to figure out my jealous reaction, but you think too highly of yourself. I am just too much of a man for Liz, and I know this." He is baiting me; he wants me to think sour grapes, and he sees this. "Why don't you ask Jeff how he would feel about Doctor Liz jumping on you like that?"

Doctor Liz appears not angry but amused. Tseng, you are losing your touch! Or wait … she wanted you to find out? It doesn't matter; she's clearly having fun. Anyways, she's never one to give up. Knowing my weakness for a wager, she says, "Let's all put in a week's pay. If we all fail, you keep all the money. But if someone succeeds, they keep it."

"Fine," I say before any of the other doctors can protest. "Three doctors. Three tests. Three guesses. Those are my conditions?"

"Make that four ... four tests," says Jeff, walking into the bar. I guess the quarantine is over.

I look over to Jeff. "You people are not the Fantastic Four and even if you are, that makes me Doctor Doom, so just leave me alone."

Jeff senses my weakness and knows he is on to something. "Let's make it more interesting. Two weeks' pay, a cancellation of the contract with the CIA and a plane ticket to anywhere you want to go if you can diagnose my brother. So what are your diagnoses?"

I am annoyed and tired. It's time for me to lash out.

"Jeff, I am not a tool or bait," I say. "I am your brother. I am also an adult and you don't need to spare my feelings by keeping your relationship with Doctor Liz a secret. Treating me like a child and disappearing for two weeks without a word is an insult. Keep me in the loop or send me back to Mississippi!" Oh did my Southern drawl just come out? I clear my throat and add, "No one is diagnosing me, because there is nothing wrong with me."

"Simple," says Liz. "Run a full genetic screening." Great; they ignore me. But I have more weapons up my sleeve. Now, on to sarcasm.

"If that is your final diagnosis, please, by all means, have fun looking for a needle in a haystack," I reply.

I turn to Doctor Greg. "Side bet: You lose and you need to make me a batch of ketamine in your lab whenever I want."

"Nice try, Tseng! You give yourself away by asking for this drug. So a disease that causes a symptom requiring a horse tranquilizer. I will go with … pain with a hint of psychosis."

"I never saw you so amused with yourself, Doctor Greg," I reply. "Funny indeed. You call me psychotic, but I am not the one playing mad scientist in your lab with Doctor Chris. I know you are trying to cure yourself of AIDS, but in the process you will kill yourself. Anyways, run your tests, but before you go through with your experiments, let me know so I can send word to your mother that her son committed suicide."

Chris, uncomfortable, changes the subject: "Run a tox screen." Foolish idea, I think. Ah, well, it will make for entertaining reading.

"Maybe parasites or a vitamin deficiency?" says Liz. "No," says Jeff. "It's cancer."

"It's time," says the redhead. "I hope two weeks was enough for you to make all the preparations?"

Tiffany looks nervous and Jeff remains cool.

He replies, "Jim is in position and the rest of the team are already on a bus out of the city."

The redhead looks tired, but she gathers her strength and stands up to face her subordinates.

"There is a tumor in our organization and it is time to find it and cut it out." As she says this, she moves over to the drawers and pulls one open. She puts away her stethoscope and pulls out a 9mm Beretta. "This will be my last mission as you both are well aware of my condition." There are no tears in Tiffany's or Jeff's eyes, but the moment is sad, as if in mourning for a fallen soldier. Jeff walks over to her and helps put her Kevlar on and fits her with a Walther PPK pistol by her ankle in an almost seductive dance. If I didn't know any better, I'd say the two might have had a romantic history.

Her voice steady, Sarah addresses the room: "Tiffany, you will remain behind, unseen, and observe. No one knows your identity, so you'll be our eyes and ears in Prague. Jeff, you are in charge effective immediately. The senior staff has been informed that I am on sabbatical. Do not discuss anything else with your superiors until all the cancer cells are removed. We don't have the luxury of a relapse."

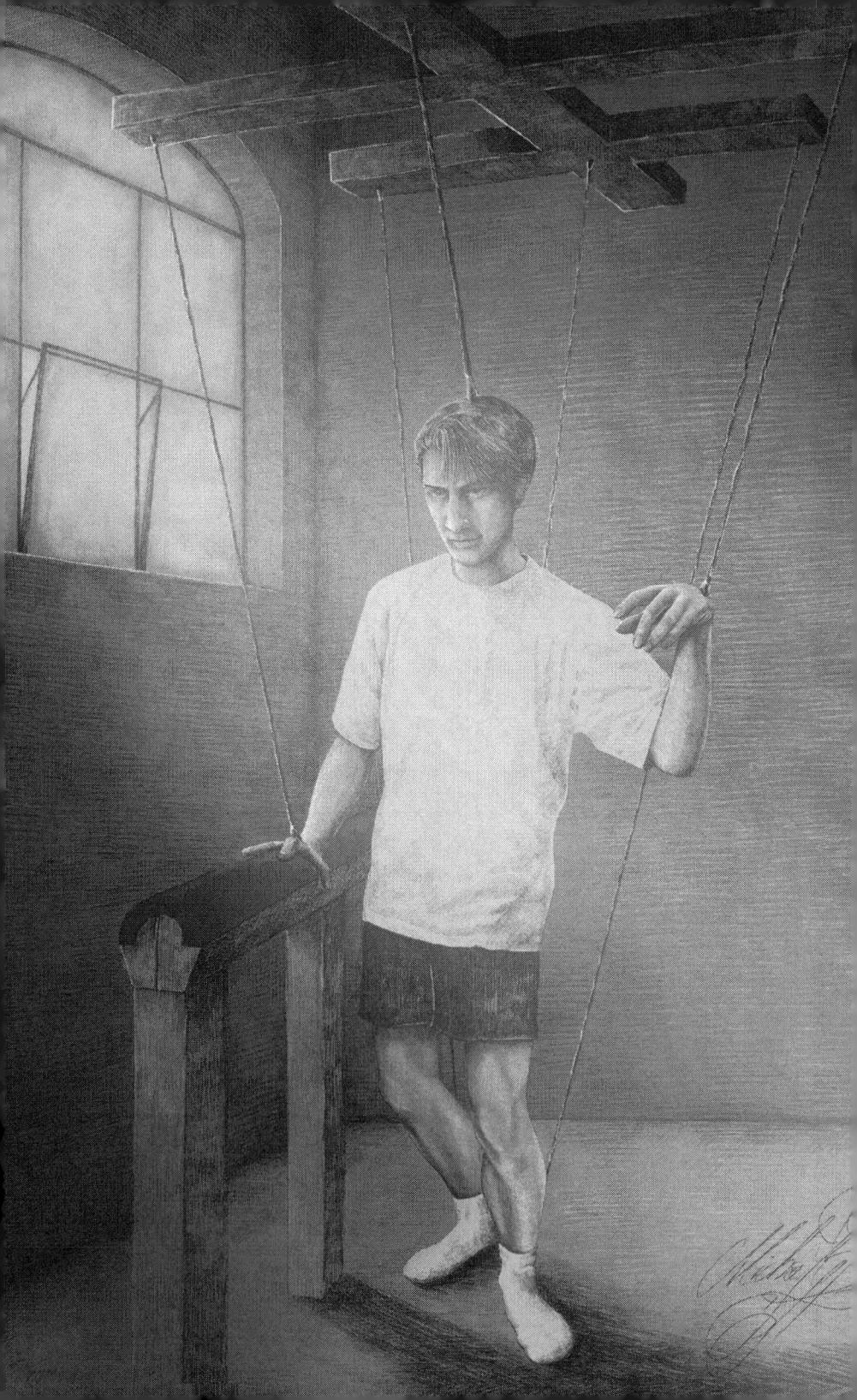

# CHAPTER XIV

# GAME OVER

"TSENG! TSENG! MEDIC! MEDIC! DIG him out. Fuck!"

My eyelids are moved up and a light is shone into them. Fucking Jeff, why is he yelling at me? No response, but I am alive. I know it. I hear the roar of a helicopter overhead. I am roughly strapped into an immobilizer gurney and airlifted. The sounds of gunfire ring out in the background.

"We are discharging you."

Another voice, most likely my superior. "From the hospital?" I ask.

"No, from service." "Honorably?" I ask. The silence says it all.

"You put yourself and your team at risk by providing medical aid to an enemy combatant. An RPG collapsed the roof above you. You and your team are lucky to be alive."

Papers are handed to me and I sign them.

"That is all, soldier. Thank you for your service."

I am sick. I know. But I'm trying to get better. The paralysis is not complete. There is a twitch here and there. Sometimes, I think I can feel them. But maybe it's in my head. Well, apparently, many things are in my head. As Einstein puts it, time is relative, and it is more relative when you've been as ill as I am for as long as I can remember.

Some things I know for sure. I did study medicine. When? The days blend into weeks and weeks into months and the months into, well, many more months when you are on opiates. I've been on them so long I don't know what is real and what is fiction. And, to be honest, I really don't care. I am on this roller coaster and there seems to be no way off of it. And that's why I'm here. The Horkých pivní sanatorium on the Vltava river, about 40 kilometers outside of Prague.

It's like something out of an old movie. Weary Czechs steam themselves in saunas and soak themselves in the thermal water. Attractive nurses hurry to and fro. And even the sick and dying drink beer. This place could be fun. Under other circumstances.

Jim isn't with me this time. I like Jim, but he never talks to me. He is normally my shadow, but not my side-kick. He looks at me not with disgust but with … pity? No. I've seen this look with Jeff. It is guilt. There is another puzzle to solve here, but do I want to solve it?

"Tseng! Tseng!"

I look up. Sarah, the mysterious redhead in scrubs, is shouting at me. She is harsh. But she is encouraging, probably because she is easy on the eyes. Her beauty doesn't matter at this moment as I hate interventions. I hate being here. Why won't my colleagues just leave me alone? My hands clutch at the metal bar. I try to stand. But I fall back. The chair is there for me. It has my backside. It's secure. The room spins. But I stay conscious for now. Any more fentanyl patches and I'll need a ventilator.

I close my eyes.

"What will you do now?"

Ah, of course; in my greatest pain and trial, I hear my brother's voice.

"The same as you, brother," I reply. "We always seem to end up together one way or another."

But this conversation is not real. Or is it? Damn memories are popping up whenever it is convenient for them.

"I just want you to know it wasn't your fault this happened, and you know I will follow you to the ends of the earth." My brother's voice ... or is it mine?

"Earth to Tseng! Wake up!" screams Sarah.

Why is she shouting? Why does she care? It doesn't matter; and why is she so beautiful? Too bad her hair is in a bun. There's something about that face. I wonder how she'd look with her hair out.

"Up!" she shouts. This time I do it. I'm standing! But I can't walk. I sit again.

"No, Tseng!" she shouts. She looks tired. Wears tinted glasses indoors. Mid thirties but seems older than her age.

Third time. I'm up. I clutch both hands to the bar. And then SNAP. Sarah handcuffs my left wrist to the bar. The chain is short. If I tried to sit down now, I'd rip my arm off. But the cuff can slide along the bar. So I try to walk. If I get to the end, it will unhook. Sarah follows me with the chair, making encouraging noises.

I'm walking. Slow. Shaky. Agonizing. Exhausting. Like a baby taking its first step. But an old, grumpy baby who needs a drink. Screw it. I will make it. I have no choice. But I need to stop. I'm angry now. And when I'm angry, well, sometimes I can't help myself.

"Sarah! Unchain me now!"

"Bet you say that to all the girls," she says. "No. You're doing this. Come on. Just four steps to go!" Wait, there is something familiar about her, or her tactics. What nurse starts off as enemy, then charms her way to being friends in seconds? Damn it, Tseng, you are getting played; better figure out who she is.

"YOU!" I say. "What do you know? Skinny for your age. Yellow-tinted glasses. Red eyes from marijuana? No, I'm going to go with yellow. Yellow from jaundice. Your clothes are slightly too big. You've lost weight very suddenly. You have cancer. Pancreatic. Why do you care about me?"

"And you're an asshole," she retorts. "The thing about you that makes people drawn to you is also the reason you push people away. Now come on. Four steps to go!"

She speaks as if she knows me. Think, Tseng, think—the familiarity, who is she? Authority, confidence, an aura of power. I realize that there's no way this woman's gonna crack. I try to take another step. As I'm halfway through, I laugh breathlessly and tell her, "Pleasure finally meeting you. Should I call you Director?"

A gunshot explodes, shattering the window of the small room. Sarah lunges toward me, and deftly unlocks the cuffs. We fall to the floor as two more shots ring out.

Lying beside me, Sarah instinctively reaches for her gun in the holster around her leg. I feel her torso, which is hard and rigid—form-fitting Kevlar. Wait, where is Jim, my bodyguard? And what type of nurse wears Kevlar? You already solved that riddle, you idiot. The shots are random. Aimed at us, but missing by far. Whoever it is knows we're in this room, but they're still far off. But I hear running footsteps. "We need to get out of here," says Sarah, looking strained.

Reaching out with a wasted arm, she grabs the frame of my wheelchair and pulls it toward me. Knowing she's too weak to help me up, I use all my strength to force myself into the seat. She stands, grabs hold of the railings, and we scramble out of the door. A bullet smashes into the wall right where we'd been standing.

This place is huge. A long corridor. Gray carpet. Dark wooden walls. We try a door at random. Locked. Sarah is panting, running out of breath. She won't be able to keep this up much longer. The corridor turns, and then we're met with a large wooden door. If it's locked, we're finished.

CRACK. A bullet smashes into the wood, right over Sarah's head. She falls to the ground. Is she hit? No blood from what I can see. Maybe she fainted. Exhaustion. I grab her gun, wheel myself around, and look into the face of the assassin.

He looks familiar. "Joe?" I ask.

"That's me," he says, in his Texan drawl. "Thanks for the diagnosis. Who would have thought it was simply mononucleosis?"

Great, I cured my assassin. I try to fire at him, but the safety is still on.

"You shouldn't have come back here, Tseng," Joe says. He lifts his left hand, revealing a gun, and pulls the trigger.


*To be continued ...*

Made in the USA
Middletown, DE
09 February 2021

33436122R00084